HEAD OVER HEELS

A STEAMY SINGLE DAD ROMANTIC COMEDY

SERENA BELL

JMG
JELSBA
MEDIA
GROUP

To Liz, who taught me to love camping and how to sing all the best trail songs.

1

LIV

E ve is handing me tissues as fast as she can pull them out of the tissue box, and I'm soaking them with my tears.

Don't worry. No one has died. Well, no people or pets have died.

Just Ethel, my twenty-year-old Honda Accord.

And technically she's not *dead*. Just... very sick.

She needs new shocks, new struts, and not one, but two brake line replacements.

Which shouldn't be a shock, because I have deferred maintenance on Ethel about as long as it's humanly possible to defer anything.

"Apparently I'm lucky to have made it this far," I wail, through my tears.

Eve hands me another tissue and gives me a big hug, which is a very loyal thing to do because I'm a snotty mess. I don't think I'd hug me if our situations were reversed.

Eve, typically, is not a mess of any kind. Her honey-colored corkscrew curls are loose in a puff around her head, but otherwise, she looks like she's on her way to work—dressed to kill in a blouse and pencil skirt and heels. Eve is an incredibly successful Realtor, Revere Lake's youngest, and part of why she's so good at what she does is that she's always on the job, even when she's theoretically relaxing.

"Three thousand dollars!" I say, for about the thirtieth time. When the mechanic said "three," I thought she meant three hundred. My knees went weak when she clarified.

"Or you could buy a used car, like Ginny said."

Ginny, the mechanic, is a friend of Eve's. She's tiny with a blond ponytail and blue eyes, ginormous coveralls and her name stitched on the pocket. When she came out of the garage bay wiping her hands on a greasy rag, I loved her instantly for messing with every mechanic stereotype I'd ever had.

Then I hated her, for destroying my carefully constructed denial about Ethel's readiness for our trip.

I was supposed to be in the garage to get a "clean bill of health for a long solo drive."

Now I know that that's like getting a full body scan and then being bummed when the radiologist tells you they've found something.

I glare daggers at Eve for daring to mention getting rid of Ethel.

"I know." Eve takes my hand in both of hers and squeezes. "I know how you feel about Ethel."

I bought Ethel with the money I hoarded and saved from the odd jobs I did the last four years I was in foster care. She was my escape from my shitty childhood, and she's taken me from town to town every time I've needed to get moving again. With Ethel in my corner, I've always known I could leave when I needed to.

Until now.

I sniff, swipe, and manage to mostly dry myself off.

"Seriously, though, babe, you should probably get a new car. Didn't Ginny say that even if you deal with Ethel's issues, she's going to be a money pit for you?"

"Yessss," I wail.

"Wait," Eve says, holding up a finger. She grabs her phone.

"What are you doing?"

"I had an idea." She tap-tap-taps, then beams up at me. "I knew it! I have a client who's moving across the country, and they're trying to unload their third car—"

"Who needs three cars!"

"It's their dump car," Eve says.

I roll my eyes. "It's probably *really* smelly."

"Ethel wasn't exactly roses and lavender," Eve points out gently. "Anyway, they say they'll take fifteen hundred for it."

For the first time since Ethel was declared mostly DOA, I feel vaguely hopeful. Heartbroken, but hopeful. Because as much as I don't want to consign Ethel to the scrap heap, I do want to get out of Revere Lake.

Enough to sacrifice Ethel in the process.

"Okay," I say grudgingly. "Tell them I'll take it. If they can be flexible on timing."

"I'll negotiate with them," she says proudly—and I know she will. Eve could negotiate Santa out of his beard. "You can plan to stay long enough to earn the money—"

"I don't have a job," I point out (not for the first time in this conversation).

"True, but you could get one. And you could stay with me." At my instant frown, she says, "I know you don't want to sleep on my shitty pullout...."

"Amen! You should sooo replace that thing."

We have a brief staring contest. I lose.

"It's not your couch that keeps me from wanting to camp with you," I say. "It's your traffic volume."

Eve chuckles. "You're just jealous."

"I'm not jealous. My girl parts get tired just thinking about it."

Eve has a *lot* of male visitors. So when I stay at her place for more than a few nights, the sound effects from her bedroom—in conjunction with the very poky metal springs of her pullout—keep me awake.

"Well, if you don't want to stay with me, you could stay with Rodro and Camilla. Their couch doesn't suck."

"It would be super awkward to ask them that, now that they have a new nanny. And awkward for her, too."

But Eve and I both know that I'm just slinging words now. It's not that I don't want to stay with her. It's not that I don't want to stay with Rodro and Camilla.

It's that I don't want to stay, period.

It's time to go.

I don't like to stay anywhere too long. I've been here almost three years and it's about a year too long for my tastes. I've been like this as long as I can remember, ever since I left my last foster home and started to live on my own. I like to be somewhere about two years and then I want to go-go-go. I'm a turtle that carries its shell on its back.

You can psychoanalyze the shit out of me, but the bottom line is that if I have to stay anywhere too long, I start to feel trapped. Itchy. Unable to sit still. Nothing tastes good or feels fun.

Until I pack my bags, load up Ethel, and set out for a new town.

"You could stay with Kieran," Eve suggests.

"No."

"Are you going to let him visit you at all?"

Kieran's the guy I'm dating and he's gotten a little too serious, starting to talk about how maybe he can come visit me in Colorado after I move there.

"He did ask."

"And you said?"

"I gave him a non-answer. I hedged."

She rolls her eyes. "No shock there."

In general, I don't keep people when I move around. The only exception is Eve. Eve and I met working at a roast beef restaurant in Salem, Massachusetts, which was the first place I went when I left my last foster home. We became fast friends, and years later, after Eve moved to Revere Lake to be close to her sister, Camilla, and Camilla's husband Rodro, Eve convinced me to come be their nanny. Getting another chance to spend time with Eve has been the best thing about staying so much longer than I meant to in Revere Lake.

"You gonna let *me* visit you?"

"Of course!"

"There's no 'of course' about it, and you know it," she says.

She knows my philosophy better than anyone. You can't hold onto people as you move around. I tried it a couple of times at first, hanging onto friends from each place I'd been —but it just didn't work for me. It always hurt when the long distance friendships got more and more stretched thin, then snapped like old elastic bands. So I quit doing it, to save all of us the wear and tear.

"What about Chase?" she demands.

"What *about* Chase?"

"Will you let *him* visit you?"

"Chase doesn't want to visit me," I scoff.

She raises her eyebrows.

"What!? He doesn't."

"You guys are pretty good friends."

I shrug.

Her eyebrows are still way up.

"At least admit you'll be bummed to leave him behind."

I shrug again.

She shakes her head. "You'll be bummed."

Chase is a friend of Eve's brother-in-law, Rodro, and somehow, against all odds, he and I have gotten to be friends, too. Despite our many differences of opinion, he and I get each other in a way I don't feel like a lot of people get me. We're also weirdly similar in some ways—like the dating thing. Chase goes through women like water, and while I'm more of a serial monogamist, long-term is never my plan. Because of the whole not-staying thing.

"You could stay with Chase," she suggests.

"Oh, because his traffic volume is so much lower than yours!?"

She grins at that. "Okay, maybe not, but he has a guest room with a semi-decent bed."

I've slept on that bed a few times when I've hung out at Chase's and fallen asleep on his couch. Or had too many glasses of wine. It's true; it's a nice bed.

"Not gonna happen," I say. "Chase and I would kill each other if we lived under one roof."

"Then I guess you're stuck with me," Eve says. "At least until you can earn enough money to buy a new car."

I nod, but I'm still not ready to accept it. The itchiness is already twining itself around my body, working its way under my skin.

I have to find a way to get out of Dodge faster.

2

CHASE

"No, no, no, Daddy! Don't go!"

I very gently peel my five-year-old daughter, Katie, off my leg and kneel. She hurls herself into my arms, and I give her a big, reassuring hug. "Celia's going to stay with you and play."

Katie lifts her face from my chest and peeks at Celia, then buries her face again. "No!"

"And I'll be back before you even know it. We'll have special dinner tonight. I'll get takeout spaghetti. And Liv's coming over to say—"

I stop myself just in time. My friend Liv's leaving tomorrow for Colorado, which sucks for many reasons, including the fact that Katie really likes her. I'd been about to say "to say goodbye."

Unfortunately for me, Katie is smart, and her memory is iron clad. She looks up, face tear-streaked. "No!" she says. "I don't want Liv to go!"

Oh, bloody hell, *bad* choice, Chase.

Katie releases a fresh storm of tears.

"Katie, hon, let's watch *Frozen*," Celia offers cajolingly.

As grateful as I am for any intervention, I wish Celia, Katie's newest nanny, had some other tricks up her sleeve. The last few mornings, it's been *Frozen* every morning, and while I know it'll work, I'm bummed that Celia isn't more creative. What about crafts or, I don't know, Candy Land? Or a book? At this point, I'd even take a new movie. Katie has seen *Frozen* so many times that she has it memorized.

But as usual, it works like a charm. Katie lets go of me and follows Celia back toward the television.

I stand for a moment, watching her go, and wondering if I'm doing something wrong. Wishing I could ask Thea whether this used to happen when she left for work. The crazy thing is that when Thea was alive and I had Katie only on rare occasions, you couldn't have paid me enough to ask a question like that, one that would have revealed my insecurities and doubts. Now that she's gone, I wish I could have an hour of her time to download everything she knew about Katie.

That'll never happen. Thea's knowledge of Katie died with her, and all Katie has is me—flailing my way through single fatherhood, doing my best not to screw it up.

I force myself to let it go for now, leaving Katie in Celia's competent, if unimaginative, hands, and head out to the car.

I tell myself I'm probably just jumpy because today's the day that Mike—my boss and the owner of Mike's Mountainwear, the outerwear retailer where I work—has promised to give me an answer about whether he will sell the shop to me when he retires.

I need to keep my eyes on that prize, because it's the key

to making sure I can give Katie the financial security she deserves. With the money Thea left Katie and the money I've saved, I can put down enough on the business to make it mine—and eventually, Katie's. Assuming Mike agrees to sell it to me.

I park in front of the store and head inside, where I'm intercepted by my friend Brooks.

"What's up with the big boy clothes?" he demands.

I'm wearing a button-down shirt and a pair of khakis. It's hardly a suit-and-tie, but Brooks is right that it's unusual for me. My usual is jeans and a fishing t-shirt. *It's fish o'clock somewhere* is my favorite.

"Mike promised me an answer by today."

Brooks claps me on the back. "Excellent."

Brooks is one of my closest friends, a co-worker and a fishing buddy. He's a pain in the ass and the most loyal, awesome guy I know. And he's been nothing but supportive of my plan to buy the store, in part because he knows it also guarantees him employment for a lot longer than if Mike closes it when he retires.

Brooks eyes me. "You nervous?" he asks.

"Nah."

"Yeah, you are." Brooks never minces words or spares anyone's feelings, which I appreciate about him. "You're nervous. Don't be. You got this. Who better than you to take over? Mike doesn't have kids, and he loves the shit out of you."

Maybe so, but Brooks is right, too: I'm nervous. Mike and I didn't get off to the best start when I began working at the store years ago, and even though I've changed a lot recently, I wonder if that first impression will keep him from thinking I'm responsible enough for the job.

I look around for Mike, and Brooks catches my wandering gaze. "He's in the back," he says.

I head there, and find him sitting at his desk, messing with spreadsheets. Mike's balding, with a round face, gray fringe over his ears, and a mustache. Today he's wearing jeans and a button down flannel shirt.

He looks up when I come in, and I don't like the look that crosses his face. It's not the look of a guy who's about to deliver good news. It's the look of a guy who's about to let you down easy.

Shit.

Mike rises, but doesn't meet my eyes.

"Chase," he says.

That's the voice of a guy who's about to let you down easy, too.

I'm a big fan of Mike. When he was actively managing the store, he ran a tight ship, and I always knew exactly what he expected from me. When he put me in charge, he made it clear that he trusted me to make decisions, and he's stayed mostly of out my way. Can't ask for a better situation. Plus when Katie came into my life, he was a saint about my working shorter hours while I sorted out child care.

"Look," he says.

I don't think any welcome sentence ever started with the word, *look*.

"If it were just up to me—"

Ugh.

"—I'd sell the shop to you. But here's the thing."

Why is there always a *thing*?

"My wife's sister's son. My nephew, sort of, I guess."

I'm realizing that whatever Mike's about to say, he doesn't seem any more excited about it than I am. So maybe that's good news. Maybe it's not a done deal, whatever it is.

"He wants the store. And my wife, she wants me to sell it to him."

My stomach goes leaden with dread. I feel the whole weight of being the only thing between Katie and the world. I want so badly to do right by her. And this store—it was my plan A, B, and C. It's what I love and what I'm good at.

There's no plan D.

Which means I have to convince Mike to sell it to me. Somehow.

I open my mouth to make my pitch—not that I have any fucking idea what it'll be, but I'm hoping something brilliant will pop out—but Mike starts talking before I can.

"She and I had a knock-down drag-out about this whole thing. Almost destroyed my marriage. I may never get laid again."

Not an image I needed to contemplate. Yikes.

"Her whole thing is, she can't tell her sister I'm selling the store to a virtual stranger when I could sell it to her kid. And I'm like, I can sell it to whoever I fucking want to, which is you." He points at me. "And she's like, 'Yeah, but I need something I can tell my sister so it doesn't ruin our relationship.' Which I get, kind of. Right?"

I'm not sure I completely followed all of that logic, but I nod.

"So I tell her, What if I prove to you that Chase is the better choice? In a way your sister can't argue with? And she said, Okay, if you can do that, I'm in." He crosses his arms. "I don't know if you know this, but I went to business school with a guy, a close friend, and he's a business plan consultant. He was the one who helped me with mine in the old days, and periodically I'll bring him back in to help me out of a bind. So I'm thinking, if you and my nephew each did a business plan, I could have him look at both plans and pick the best one. *Voilà*. No marital disaster, and the store ends up in the best hands."

I hate this plan. For many reasons. Not the least of which is, I only barely know what a business plan is.

"So what do you think? You and Whitaker each—"

"Wait. Your nephew's name is Whitaker?"

"Yeah," Mike says. "My wife's family is very—you know." He tips his nose up, to indicate haughtiness. "My nephew graduated from Yale and then went to Wharton Business School."

"Whoa," I say. "The guy I'm competing with to buy your store went to Wharton Business School?"

To be totally honest, I don't know anything about Wharton Business School, except that it's one of the really big deal ones. Like Yale is a really big deal place to go to college.

But I do know when I'm in over my head, and this is definitely one of those times. No way I can win a business plan contest against a guy named Whitaker who went to Yale and Wharton Business School.

Mike crosses his arms. "You know I want to see this store go to someone who loves it. Who appreciates it. Who will take care of it," he says. "You gotta do this, Chase."

I almost say, *because you don't want to stand up to your wife and your wife doesn't want to stand up to her sister*, but I stop the words just in time from popping out. It doesn't matter what the family dynamics are. Everyone knows you can't win that game, and I know it better than anyone.

But that doesn't mean I have to spend weeks of my life developing a business plan just so I can lose the store to Mike's wunderkind nephew. I've played this game and lost before; I don't need to be told again that I'm not good enough.

"I don't know," I say.

"Think about it, huh?" Mike says sternly.

"I will," I say, by which I mean, I probably won't.

I'M in a craptastic mood the rest of the day. Even Brooks seems to know to steer clear of me all morning. But at lunch he corners me. "What's going on?"

"Nothing."

"Is he going to sell you the store? Or not?"

"Uh, it's not that simple."

"What's not that simple?"

"He wants me to do a business plan contest with his nephew, and whoever wins can buy the store."

"Huh," Brooks says.

"And his nephew graduated from Yale and Wharton Business School."

"Oh, yeah, geez," Brooks says. "What the fuck can you do against that?"

"Right?" I say.

Still, even though I was having the same thought myself, it galls me that all it takes to win this fight is two overpriced degrees.

"What?" Brooks asks.

"Nothing," I say. "Just... thinking."

Maybe I will take Mike up on the chance to try to outgun his nephew.

Brooks raises an eyebrow. "Thinking about taking on the man?" he asks.

"Something like that."

When it's time to close up, Brooks invites Rodro and me for drinks, but neither of us can go. I promised Katie takeout, and Rodro says Camilla will kill him if he doesn't get home to help with the kids. Brooks says, "All my friends have fucking kids. How did this happen? I need new friends."

"Alternatively, you need to fall in love, get married, and have kids," Rodro says.

"Not gonna happen," Brooks says.

"How's Sawyer doing?" I ask. Sawyer is Brooks's brother. His wife died last year, and he's a single dad, too. We're in similar boats, both having lost the mothers of our kids. Only Sawyer has it way worse than I do, because he was head over heels for his wife, and Thea and I were barely speaking.

"Meh," Brooks says. "He's like a zombie. Walking around, carrying on conversations, but mostly dead."

I feel a pang of deep sympathy for the guy. "Tell him if he wants to hang sometime, I'm game."

"I'll tell him." Brooks' voice is grim, like he doesn't think that'll ever happen.

I say goodbye to my friends and head to the car. On the way, I text Liv. *Any chance you're free? Katie would love to see you.*

I get behind the wheel and my phone buzzes.

Shitty day, she texts back.

Consolation party?

Consolation party is a thing Liv and I do, usually after one or both of us has been on a crappy date. We meet up and watch movies on two separate devices. That's because we can never agree on a movie. Ever.

Sure. Want me to pick up takeout?

That would be 100% awesome. Anything for me, but I promised Katie spaghetti.

On it.

Traffic sucks on the way home, and by the time I pull into the driveway in front of the house where Katie and I live, I'm dead tired and I've decided there's definitely no point to my entering a business plan contest that's going to take more of my time away from Katie and probably lead nowhere.

I push open the front door and...

"Let It Go" wails its way into my brain.

Frozen is on the fucking television.

Again.

How many times has Celia let Katie watch *Frozen* today?

Celia herself is sitting in the big armchair in the living room. It isn't till I get close that I realize she's asleep. And then I realize that she's asleep with her hand wrapped around something.

It's a flask.

I very gently pry the flask out of her hand and sniff it.

Holy *shit*.

Celia opens her eyes. I stare at her. She stares back at me, at the flask in my hand, under my nose. Whiskey scented, unmistakably—not that I thought the flask would be full of water.

"I, uh, guess you probably want me to go." She slurs her words a little.

"Yeah," I say. "And take any of your stuff that's here with you."

She hauls herself out of the chair and heads upstairs.

I'm reeling, heart suddenly pounding half out of my chest. I think of all the times in the last few months that I couldn't find something I was sure I had. A bottle of wine, a last can of beer, that bottle of vodka in the freezer. Now it all makes sense. And it could have been so much worse. Celia has a car, and she frequently drives Katie around. To the grocery store, to the playground—all over the place.

How many times has she driven Katie drunk?

I can't let myself think about it.

I sink into the couch next to my daughter. "Hey, Katie girl," I say, pushing her hair out of her eyes. Kissing her on her satiny soft cheek. I love this girl so much. It's hard for me to reconcile how much time I wasted not being in her life because of my pride and stupidity. I mean, yes, I saw her occasional weekends... but not nearly enough.

"Hey, Daddy," Katie says, too blissed out on *Frozen* to give me anything else.

I wonder if part of why Katie was weird about being left with Celia was that even as a five-year-old, she sensed that something was not quite right?

Celia comes back down the stairs with her suitcase. I've called her an Uber. I tell her Katie and I will drive her car to her house and take the Uber back to ours.

As I'm outlining the plan, I realize I owe her money. Do you pay the drunk nanny for her last week of work? Deciding to err on the side of generosity, I write the check and hand it to her. Her hand closes over it, but I don't release it.

"You need to get help. Please get help."

Celia's startled gaze flips to mine. Has no one ever told her that before? It seems possible.

I round Katie up and we follow Celia out.

Holy shit, this day sucks.

3

LIV

When I show up with Chase and Katie's takeout, Katie answers the door.

"Hi, Livvy. I'm watching *Frozen*," the world's most adorable five-year-old proclaims proudly, pushing strands of blond hair out of her face. The strands fall back into her eyes, and I kneel to tuck them behind her ears.

"What part are you at?"

"Elsa's ice palace. She's singing 'Let It Go.'" Katie sings a few lines, twirling wildly around the living room, arms thrown out. She finishes with a curtsy.

I stifle a giggle. "That's my favorite part. I brought you spaghetti." I display the brown takeout bag.

"Yum, sketti!"

Katie turns her attention back to the unfurling grandeur of Elsa's ice palace.

I head toward the kitchen. Chase's house, as usual, is trashed. Not that it's dirty—just scattered all over with toys and *stuff*. One of the reasons I told Eve staying at Chase's house wouldn't work for me.

Still, showing up here always feels like finally pulling on sweats and taking off my makeup at the end of a long day. It's super comfy. Not my style at all, or really any style—a mishmash of well-worn furniture and rugs—but the whole thing feels a lot like wrapping up in a fleece blanket and watching a good chick flick. Which I've done maybe a hundred times on Chase's armchair by now, while he watches his action movies on his own laptop on the couch a couple of feet away. It's our ritual.

"Hey," Chase says, coming out of the kitchen.

He looks like absolute hell. I mean, he looks gorgeous, because Chase is, no doubt about it, a gorgeous man. He has beautiful brown eyes, flecked with darker brown, gold, and green, fringed with long eyelashes. But right now they have circles under them.

"You okay?" I ask him. I've had a hell of a day myself, but he looks worse than I feel.

He brushes his hand through his reddish-brown hair, making it all stand on end. Chase has that kind of not-quite curly hair that won't behave, but because he's a guy, no one gives a shit. When he rumples it up and it's all over the place, he looks hot. I say that objectively, because I can appreciate a hot guy, not because I personally crush on Chase. I know most people don't think men and women can be just friends —I used to believe that until I met Chase—but they really *can*.

"Not so much," he says.

"What's up?"

"Just got back from driving the nanny's car to her house. I had to fire her."

"What?!"

"She was asleep on a chair with a flask in her hand when I got home. Whiskey. And Katie was watching *Frozen*, which was also true when I left this morning."

"Oh. That sucks."

"You have no idea."

"What are you going to do?"

"I don't know." He runs his fingers through his hair again.

"You need me to watch her tomorrow?"

He raises his gaze, which has been on the floor, to me, and brightens a little. "Would you do that?"

"Sure," I say. "Turns out I'm stuck here for a bit, anyway."

"Wait, what?" he asks.

"Ethel died. Well, she didn't die. But she's on life support. It'll cost some ungodly amount to fix her. Or I can buy a used car for fifteen hundred. Either way, I need money before I can get to Colorado."

"So, you're gonna... what?"

"Crash with Eve."

"On the couch of death?"

"Yeah. I just hope she doesn't bring anyone home. Those walls are thin."

Chase grimaces. "Fun, fun, fun. Well, if you can't sleep, we can both be insomniacs."

"You been up a lot at night?"

"Katie's not sleeping great," he admits. "She's fine during the day, mostly, but she's having a lot of nightmares. And a lot of times when I wake up, I can't fall asleep again."

My heart squeezes for both of them. Even though Chase and Thea didn't get along great, I know Katie's grief is hard on him.

He starts unpacking the takeout bags I brought.

"What is this?" he demands.

I hide my smile. Messing with Chase about takeout is one of my favorite sports. "Sushi."

"Seriously? Whatever happened to, you know, pizza? Chinese? Burgers and fries?"

I hide a smile. "It's summer. And sushi has lots of omega-3 fats. It's healthy. And beautiful."

"Beautiful," he mutters. "Food is not supposed to be beautiful. It's supposed to taste good."

Just so you know, Chase likes to pretend he's surly and mean, but he's the biggest softie on earth. You just have to watch him for three seconds with Katie to see it.

I carefully transfer my sushi to a plate.

"Don't do that! It just makes more dishes!"

My turn to shrug. We have this argument all the time. I've got this thing for making meals as homey as possible. It's another side effect of growing up in foster homes. There was a lot of grab-and-go in my life, and I love the idea of eating with plates and silverware and napkins and all that jazz.

I dump Katie's spaghetti into a bowl and he says, "Now that looks good."

"It's Katie's." I warn him off with a glare.

He sighs. "I'm never letting you order the takeout again."

While I finish setting the table—which involves first shoveling all the crap *off* the table and trying to organize it into piles that make some sense—Chase goes into the living room, shuts off the movie, and comes back into the kitchen with Katie at his side.

I set the bowl of spaghetti, heated, in front of her. She takes one look at it and bursts into tears.

"What's wrong, baby?" Chase asks.

"Mommy always cut my sketti," Katie wails.

Chase looks utterly stricken, and I can't really blame him. He starts to form words, but I know nothing he says now is going to help. At all. I know the only thing that will help—aside from the one thing neither of us has any power to do, which is to bring Thea back.

"She's hungry," I murmur to Chase. "Let's get some food into her."

I take a knife and fork and begin slicing the spaghetti into shorter pieces, and Katie's wails soften immediately.

"Take a bite, hon," I tell Katie.

She does. Then another. Until she's shoveling it in. She's still sniffling a bit, but no longer crying.

"Slow down, hon."

"It's really good," she says, through a mouthful. "It's the best sketti ever."

Chase's face slowly relaxes. His shoulders, too.

"She didn't realize how hungry she was because she was watching the movie, and now she's too hungry to have any resilience. She'll be fine. Right, Katie girl? You're fine, aren't you?"

She smiles around her spaghetti, sauce smudged in a ring around her mouth.

Chase mouths something at me.

Thank you.

"It's nothing," I murmur.

He shakes his head. "Right now," he says, "it's everything."

Chase comes downstairs after putting Katie to bed and collapses dramatically on the couch.

"That bad?"

"No," he says. "She was actually pretty sleepy and cooperative. This day just needs to end."

"You want me to leave?"

He shakes his head. "No. Stay."

"Was it just the nanny thing?"

He shakes his head.

"What else?"

"You know how I want to buy the store?"

I nod.

"Well, Mike wants to sell it to me, but his wife wants to sell it to her sister's kid. So Mike decided it would be a great idea to set up a business plan contest between the two of us, judged by a friend of his who's a business plan expert."

"Sounds reasonable," I say.

"Yeah, I guess, except the sister's kid is a business school grad."

He looks utterly defeated, which is very un-Chase-like.
I've never seen Chase look as back-on-his-heels as he does
right now. I think of him as a self-confident, even cocky guy—
that's how come he's such a magnet for the opposite sex.

I'm not into that—the cocky thing—but if I were? He's
definitely got it in spades.

"That is kind of intense," I admit. "But just because he's
been to business school doesn't mean he actually knows how
to run a clothing store. Which you do. Absolutely. I think
you've got the inside line on this."

"Wait, really?" He looks so surprised, it surprises me. "You
think I could do it?"

"Hell, yeah," I say. "I mean, A, you know the business
inside and out. B, you have good ideas about how to fix stuff.
And C, whatever you don't know, you'll figure out, because
you've got a good head for it."

There's a small, pleased smile on Chase's face, and it does
something weird to my chest. I don't think of him as a guy who
needs his ego stroked. Ever. But apparently, when it comes to
certain things, he's less sure of himself than he seems.

Maybe I don't know Chase quite as well as I think I do.

We settle in to watch our movies. He's sitting on the couch
with his iPad and Jason Bourne, and I'm curled up in the
armchair with my iPad and *Bridget Jones's Baby*.

Odd, right? How did this parallel movie-watching ritual
ever come into existence? Excellent question.

I met Chase pretty soon after I started working for Rodro
and Camilla. I was home with their oldest—at that point only
—child while they went out for date night. Vera, the baby,
was asleep, and I was watching a movie on my laptop in the

living room. There was a knock on the front door, and I paused the movie, but before I could even get out of my chair, I heard the front door swing open.

I went dead silent. I was all alone in the house with baby Vera and not expecting Rodro and Camilla back for hours. I scanned the room wildly for a weapon, and failing to find anything suitable, grabbed my laptop from the coffee table, figuring I could clobber someone over the head or jam it into his throat.

"Rodro?" a male voice called out, quietly enough not to wake the baby.

Okay, most random burglars don't call out the name of the homeowner, or lower their voices so they don't wake the baby. My heart was still pounding like it was going to burst out of my chest, but my better instincts took over enough that I set down the laptop.

A gorgeous man appeared in the living room doorway, and let out a scream when he saw me. Like, the girliest scream on earth.

I started laughing.

"Jesus, you scared the shit out of me!" he said.

"I scared you!? You just showed up randomly and let yourself in!"

He was still clutching his pearls and panting, which only made me laugh harder. "I'm sorry. I'm Chase Crayton. I'm Rodro's friend. You are?"

I reached for my phone and texted Rodro. *Someone named Chase Crayton showed up here. Okay to let him in?*

"You're checking up on me?" he asked.

"Wouldn't you? If our situations were reversed?"

"Our situations *are* reversed," he pointed out. "But I'm not checking up on you."

"Well la-di-da. Maybe that's because you're a man and have the luxury of not fearing for your physical safety."

He looked like he was thinking that through carefully. "Maybe so," he agreed, finally. "But at least tell me who you are."

"The nanny. Olivia Stratten. Liv."

"Right," he said. "Of course. That makes total sense. Are Rodro and Camilla out?"

"Yeah."

"Shit," he said, and sank into an armchair.

Right then, a text came back from Rodro. *He's good people. Camilla says don't fall for him, though. NSFW, by which she means not safe for women.*

I looked him over. I could see that he was unsafe in that regard—way too good-looking for his own well-being. "You, um, need them? Urgently?"

His eyes met mine, whiskey brown and beautiful. "Nah. I just—had a really shitty date, and when Rodro was still single, I used to always show up at his place and rehash my shitty dates. But he's not single and I should probably get out of this habit."

"You can rehash it to me." I don't know why I said that. I guess the fact that Rodro had said he was *good people.* But also, I kind of liked him. He felt comfortable.

He looked at me for a moment longer, like he was gauging whether I'd be any good at listening to his rehash, then launched into it.

It sounded like a doozy. A setup, and it turned out that he'd already slept with her a couple of times and moved on.

But she hadn't moved on. She spent the evening trying to negotiate with him for another chance. He fled as soon as he could.

He told the story dryly, hilariously. He made himself the villain, and I couldn't help laughing—with him. Still, I added that story to what Rodro had told me Camilla had said. NSFW. I made a note. *Don't fall for him. Ever.*

(I've stuck to it, by the way.)

When he was done with the rehashing, he said, "I interrupted your movie."

"You can watch it with me if you want."

"What is it?"

"*You've Got Mail.*"

"Not a fucking chance." He pulled out his phone. "I've been meaning to watch the new Marvel movie, though. So I'll do that."

Thus was born the first ever Liv-and-Chase consolation party.

When our movies were done, he said, "I owe you one."

"What?"

"If you have a shitty date, you can rehash to me."

He took my phone and put his number in it, then texted himself.

"You should know that Camilla has already told me you're not dateable."

His eyebrows shot up. "I have to admit, that is so fucking true."

"I take advice like that very seriously."

"As well you should."

There was laughter in his eyes, and a curve to his (very lush) mouth.

A couple of weeks later, I went out on the worst date of my life (to this day), with this guy who wouldn't even make eye contact with me over dinner and could barely stammer out answers to my questions, let alone pose one of his own. I'm sure he wasn't a bad guy, just painfully socially awkward, but it was brutal.

In the car afterwards, I wanted to tell someone about it, and I thought of Chase and his offer to let me rehash to him.

Why the hell not?

I texted him and told him my story, and he texted back to say that he'd just been on a date with a woman who'd brought her cats with her in their carriers, one in each hand.

That was a waste of an evening, he texted.

Amen to that.

I would have been a lot happier at home with an action flick, a six-pack, and a large pepperoni.

Me, too, except chick flick, chocolate, and wine.

Let's do it.

Do what?

Let's have another consolation party. My place, 45 minutes, bring your own movie-playing device and snack and drink of choice.

I hesitated.

I texted back: *Just to be clear, I'm not interested in hooking up.* I didn't want to be a jerk, but I also didn't want there to be any misunderstandings. Camilla had warned me, and it was obvious that her advice was on target.

I'm all for being clear. No hookup. Just movie. I swear on the Mariners' prospects for this year.

It made me smile. Maybe because dating was so exhausting—the hope, the preparation, the anticipation, the burst bubble, the putting on the best face you can while the minutes crawl by.

Chase was offering me the opposite.

Just like that, we were friends. And we have been, for more than two years. If either of has a bad date, the other one has to come over afterward so we can debrief. We mock the bad dates relentlessly, laugh like fools, and toast our continuing single status (Chase stocks wine for me; I stock scotch for him; and we bring our own snacks, because we can't agree on them). Afterward, if it's not too late, we watch movies— sitting side by side with our iPads, earbuds in, watching our respective genres.

We get together other times, too, but for me at least, my favorite times are still those post-date bitch sessions.

I'm going to miss our get-togethers when I go.

Anyway, tonight, we're midway through our cocktail of Jason Bourne and *Bridget Jones's Baby* when Bridget Jones's baby starts crying. Only Bridget hasn't actually given birth yet, so I pause my movie and tug out my earbuds. Katie.

I look over at Chase, and he's asleep in his chair. Poor dude. I hate to wake him, not when he's been getting up with Katie so many nights, so I push myself out of my chair and head up the stairs. I push her door open and kneel beside her bed. I put my hand out to touch her hair in the dark.

"Mommy."

My heart wrings.

"It's Liv, baby. It's Liv."

Even though I know I'm not who she wants, she shushes. Thank God, because I could feel her sobs in my gut.

"You okay, Katie girl?"

"I had a bad dream."

"You're okay now." I stroke her forehead, and she settles back down. Her hair is wet from tears.

My own mother died when I was seven. I don't remember her very well. But one thing I remember vividly is that sometimes, when she left me with a babysitter she would come in late to say good night, and I would rise through the layers of sleep to the comforting feel of her cheek against mine and the scent of her shampoo in my nose.

I'm not sure if the sharp grief I feel right now is Katie's or mine.

"Had a bad dream."

"I know, Katie girl. It's okay. It was just a dream. Go back to sleep. I'll sit with you a minute." I brush Katie's hair back.

I hesitate a moment, then lie down beside her and rest my cheek against hers. She smells clean and salty-sweet. Not a baby smell, but a healthy-kid smell.

I wonder if it's how I smelled to my mother.

In the first foster home I lived in, the mom used to sit up with me when I woke from nightmares, stroking my back, telling me I'd be okay.

She smelled like nutmeg and cinnamon, whereas my real mom had smelled like vanilla. Her hands were big—hefty and reassuring—whereas my own mom's had fluttered over my hair. But she was there, and most nights, that was enough.

The first time I woke my second foster mom in the middle of the night, she told me for Christ's sake not to be such a baby, it was just a dream.

I never woke my third foster mom up. By then—age ten— I'd learned to do everything I could to be hassle free. The less trouble you caused, the more likely you'd get to stay. So I got up in the middle of the night to comfort the younger kids who woke with nightmares, not expecting anyone to comfort me.

Until Zeke, of course. Zeke comforted me when I had nightmares.

With promises he didn't keep.

Katie has turned over onto her stomach and is settling down now, hiccupping occasionally. I rub her back, listening to her breathing. Her body warms as she slips toward sleep.

She shudders once and the last bit of tension ebbs away. Her breath sighs out in sleep. I stay with her a few minutes longer, then slowly draw back my hand, willing her not to wake.

I slip out of her room and tiptoe downstairs, where I almost knock Chase over, coming up.

5

CHASE

"She okay?"

"She's fine." Liv's voice is soft. Gentle, like I might be breakable. "She had a nightmare, but she's asleep now."

"Thank you."

It's a weird feeling of relief, having someone else take care of Katie for a few minutes. Now I know how Thea felt all along, doing this on her own.

Which, to be honest, only opens the old wound, the part of me that still asks: How could Thea think so little of me that she'd rather raise Katie by herself than include me in their lives? And not only that, but how could I have wanted so much to be with Thea when she hadn't wanted to be with me?

"Chase? Where'd you go?"

"Sorry—thinking of something."

I reverse down the stairs and Liv follows me into the living room. We sit down with our iPads, but neither of us turns them on again right away. I don't know what's in her head, but I'm thinking. Not about Thea any more. About how when I woke up to find myself alone in the living room and realized Liv was upstairs with Katie, I totally trusted that she would do right by my girl.

Since Katie came to live here, Liv's been amazing with her. Like the way she was earlier, chatting with her about *Frozen*, bringing her spaghetti. And at dinner, when Katie had that meltdown over her spaghetti not being cut the way Thea did it, Liv just fixed it. No muss, no fuss.

"You're really good with her."

She shrugs.

"No, you are. She loves you."

At that moment, I realize I'm being a total dope. The answer to both our problems is right in front of our noses.

"I just had a brilliant idea," I say.

"That scares me."

I roll my eyes at her. "No, seriously, hear me out. I need a nanny. You need a job, money, and a place to stay that isn't Eve's shitty couch. Right?"

She's listening. I can see her thinking about it.

"So what if you agree to nanny Katie for two weeks and hire your own replacement during that time. I pay you fifteen hundred bucks—that's what you said a used car would cost, right?"

"Yeah."

I'm half expecting her to come back at me with all the reasons it wouldn't work—all the reasons she and I would kill each other living under one roof—but she looks thoughtful.

"It would be great to know I could still leave in two weeks." She brushes her fingers idly over the dark surface of her iPad. "And it would be even better not to have to sleep on Eve's couch."

I'm elated. I've been wondering since I escorted Celia to the door how the hell I was going to get through the next few days or maybe even weeks until I could find a replacement. Liv's staying here would be the perfect solution.

"We'd need some ground rules," Liv muses. She gives me a stern look. "No housework, no laundry, no cooking unless I decide I feel like it."

"Okay," I say.

She narrows her eyes at me.

Okay, shoot me, I'm only human. Celia had been doing my laundry, and it would have been nice if Liv kept doing it, but I'm not an idiot, either. I can do my own laundry, and for fuck's sake, it's way more important to me that Katie has someone to take care of her than that my laundry gets done.

"I will do my own laundry," I say earnestly. "And we can get takeout if you don't want to cook."

"And I only work when the store's open. The rest of the time, you're on your own."

"No problem. Oh, that reminds me: my parents are going to be here Monday night—they're stopping by on their way back from a Vancouver trip. You don't have to be here for that. You might not want to be here for that."

She shrugs. "Maybe I'll see if Eve wants to hang out or something."

"And—oh. Wait."

"What?"

"You said you're off duty when the store's closed, but I have a date this Saturday night."

She shrugs. "Yeah, I'll watch Katie then, no problem. We can call that an exception."

But suddenly—and I can't explain why this is—that feels weird. For all the times we've met up after dates we've been on with other people, it feels not-right to leave Liv here with Katie while I go out with someone. "Um, no, don't worry about it—I'll get someone else."

She levels me with a distinctly Liv look, all suspicion and scorn. "Don't get weird about it."

When I don't immediately respond, she shakes her head. "Chase, what kind of bullshit is this? We have never been weird about each other dating."

"I'm not being weird," I say. The thing is, I can't quite figure out what my issue is. I mean, it's not like I'd bring anyone back here with Katie sleeping in the house. But it's not beyond the realm of possibility that I could go home with someone and not reappear in my own house until, I don't know, four, five a.m. Walk-of-shame territory.

And what? So what? Liv's right. What's so different about doing that when Celia's sleeping in the house with Katie versus when Liv is?

Nothing. Nothing at all.

"If you are going to be weird about this, Chase Crayton, tell me now and we'll scrap the whole thing, because I will not let you mess up our friendship."

Her arms are crossed, her eyebrows drawn together in a glare.

"I'm not going to be weird about it. And you're the one who's messing up our friendship by moving to Golden."

Which sucks. Let's just put it out there. I don't want Liv to leave. Our consolation parties may be a weird tradition, but it's our weird tradition. She's already made it pretty clear that she doesn't stay in touch with people when she does her cut-and-run routine, so I haven't pushed it. And I don't even know what it would be like if we did stay in touch. Would we FaceTime our consolation parties? Seems pretty silly.

"Okay, so we're okay with the dating, right?" Liv asks, shrugging. "You go out, you get laid, you come home whenever, no biggie."

Something tweaks me about that. "I don't have sex with every woman I—"

"Sorry," she says quickly. "That was out of line. I know you don't always. I just meant I know how it is, right? Nothing is going to shock me, and I don't judge. Just go on your date, and I'll stay here with Katie."

"What about you?"

"What about me?"

"Your dating life."

Liv dates. In the time I've known her, she's gotten serious about a few guys. Or they've gotten serious about her. That's really more the case. When she breaks it off, she says stuff like:

He was starting to talk about marriage and kids.

He wanted me to spend weekends at his place.

He wanted me to leave some of my stuff at his place.

He asked if he could leave a toothbrush at my place.

It doesn't take much, actually, for Liv to run the other way. She makes fun of me for my love-em-and-leave-em habits, but she's kind of a one-woman-wrecking machine herself.

She sweeps her hair back with one hand and says, "Yeah, I'm seeing this guy, and I might go out with him on Sunday or whatever. But I never bring guys back someplace I work, so you don't have to worry about that."

Something curdles in the pit of my stomach. I'm not sure if it's "seeing this guy" or "never bring guys back someplace I work" or "you don't have to worry." Something just doesn't sit right.

Liv crosses her arms, all businesslike. "Is that it? Are we done? Because I should head home."

Ignoring the disturbance in my gut, I say lightly, "You live here. It is home."

"I gotta get Eve's car back to her. And my stuff is at her place." She thinks a minute. "Can you pick me up tomorrow morning?"

"Seven thirty?"

She winces. "Mike's doesn't open till ten."

I'd forgotten she's not a morning person. "Uh, yeah. I was thinking about going in to start working on the business plan, but if that doesn't work for you, no biggie."

"No, that's fine," she says.

I walk her to the door. I reach out to shake her hand—it feels like we should seal the deal we've made—and she leans in for our usual quick hug. Somehow we end up doing both at the same time, which means my hand gets crushed against her breast.

My brain goes into instant shutdown at the softness, like I'm thirteen and not twenty-eight, like I'm copping my first illicit feel.

Also, something about the weird way we fell into the hug puts my face in her hair, which smells amazing, like apples.

I jump back because I can feel myself getting hard, and the last thing I want is anything between us, no pun intended.

She slips out the door.

I stand there for a minute, trying to settle myself down. That was downright weird. I don't get hard for Liv.

I lock the front door and climb the stairs to make sure Katie's all tucked in. I kiss her forehead and pull her covers up, then head into my bedroom, shed my clothes, brush my teeth, and get into bed.

I congratulate myself on my good work. Katie's going to love having Liv here. And I gave Liv a temporary job and a place to live.

What's not to love?

Only: I can feel it there, still swirling in my gut, my surprised reaction to the unexpected contact between us. I've shut it down hard, but like the browser window you don't want your coworker to see, it's still open down there, somewhere.

6

LIV

hase and Katie pick me up the next morning and bring me back to the house.

"Livvy, will you braid my hair?" Katie asks me in the car. "Daddy is bad at it."

I sneak a look at Chase's face. "I am," he admits.

"How about I teach Daddy to braid your hair?" I ask her. "Because I can only stay for two weeks, and after that, you'll need him to be good at it."

"Okay," Katie says.

We set up in the kitchen, and I tell Chase to show me what he's got. Within a minute, Katie is squirming and tear-streaked, and Chase is helpless and frazzled.

"You can do this," I tell him.

It would be easy for me to take the brush and the elastic and do it for him, but that's not what I want for Chase and Katie.

"Is it brushed?"

He shakes his head. "I keep making her cry."

"The trick is to hold on to her hair above where you're brushing. So you're not pulling on her scalp."

I take the brush and show him, then hand it back to him. He gets through the rest of her hair without sending her into sobs again.

"Now put the brush down so you have both hands free," I instruct.

He sets it on the table.

"Divide her hair into three parts."

The fine corn silk of Katie's hair catches on the roughness of Chase's hands, on the tiny curls of hair below each knuckle and the callused skin of his palms.

"Right side over center, then left side over center—no, the new center. See how the right is the center now?" I step close behind him and put my hand over his. He smells fresh from the shower, and my spidey senses identify Ivory and Old Spice, two of my favorites. Funny; I guess whenever I've hung out with him before, it's been in the evening, not right after he showered.

I definitely would have noticed if he smelled this yummy.

I show him how the braid works.

"Oh!" he says. "I get it."

He winds the hanks around each other with surprising dexterity. I guess I shouldn't be surprised. Those are hands that tie flies from tiny feathers and filament strands. A braid is big work by comparison. Right over center, left over center —I realize I'm staring, almost mesmerized.

He fumbles again trying to get the elastic on, and I have to step in to show him. "Over, twist, over again. Like so."

He takes the elastic from me, and his hand brushes mine. I'm suddenly hyperaware—of that touch, but also of how male he is. It's one of those moments of attraction that happen from time to time between people, when you can feel the chemistry prickle through the air, one body speaking to another. Only, Chase's body doesn't usually—doesn't ever—do that to mine.

I shrug it off. It happens, right? You don't have to imbue every pheromone that jumps the gap with meaning.

He successfully ties off the braid, then turns to me with a grateful smile. "This is exactly what I needed," he says.

"Well, happy to provide the service."

He sets the brush down, dries Katie's tears with the bottom of his T-shirt, and gives her a big hug. "You look beautiful," he says.

I grin to myself. It's a little lumpy, but whose first braid is perfect?

"I guess I should get going."

"Yup! We'll be fine. Playground in the morning, and then we have a fun plan for the afternoon."

"Wish I could hang out with you guys instead of going to work."

"Well, you can't," I tell him, merciless. "But. You need to be home for dinner."

"What? Why?"

"Take my word for it. For Katie's sake, you won't want to miss it."

I shoo him out and help Katie into her sturdy play sandals. We head to the playground, where we keep ourselves busy most of the morning. Then I take Katie back to the house and give her a peanut-butter-and-jelly sandwich and apple slices for lunch. When she's done, I explain my shopping project.

"Your dad is a great guy," I tell her. "He only has one flaw." And then I outline his shortcomings and explain how we're going to remedy them.

She totally gets it, and she's completely on board. She's practically bouncing in her seat from excitement.

We spend most of the afternoon putting our plan into effect. We borrow Eve's car and go to Target and Pier 1—Katie is fascinated by both stores and keeps hopping from item to item. She can't believe there are stores this big with this much stuff. (I'm not sure where her mom shopped with her, but maybe she did most of her shopping when Katie was at school or activities—Chase has always told me Katie's life with Thea was very programmed.) Anyway, Katie takes her job very seriously, carefully considering every choice I give her, finally pronouncing her decisions with great ceremony.

She clearly carries the making-things-beautiful gene, even if her dad doesn't. I make a mental note to tell Chase he has to make sure to leave some room in her life for the pretty and the fussy, even if he scorns both himself. The first two foster homes where I lived were plain-Jane cozy and homey, but my third foster "mom" took Martha Stewart to the nth power—and that was where I learned to pay attention to the details. I hadn't realized anything was missing from my life before, but I really blossomed under her tutelage—learning how to cut and arrange flowers; stitch curtains, pillows, placemats, napkins, and coasters; use a hot-glue gun to embellish anything and everything, and make the small space allotted to me—just a corner of one bedroom —my own.

Next, Katie and I go to the grocery store. While we're picking produce, my phone buzzes. It's Eve.

Had an idea for someone to take over w K when u leave. Gillian Hollis. Mom she wks for lost her job & laid G off.

Gillian is Eve's friend who nannies. I met her once when the kids we were nannying for had a play date. She's terrific with kids.

And she's exceptionally pretty.

That last bit isn't relevant, of course. It just popped into my head.

"Liv!" Katie tugs on my hand. "Stop texting!"

"I'm finding you a really wonderful person to be your nanny after I move to Golden."

"What's her name?"

"Her name is Gillian."

"That is the prettiest name I ever heard!" Katie says, beaming.

I should probably be sad that I'm so easily replaced, but the truth is, whatever makes this easiest for Katie—and Chase—is what I want. I text Eve back.

She would be perfect.

She's in Chicago at her parents'. Back last wk Aug. There's a contact attached to the text.

"Give me one more minute," I tell Katie. "I want to text Gillian and arrange for her to come meet you before it slips my mind."

This causes Katie to bounce up and down on her toes in the middle of the berry section.

I drop Gillian a text, and Katie and I finish up at the grocery store.

We head home and put our plan into action.

When Chase comes through the door at the end of the day, we're ready for him.

"Daddy!" she crows. "We made a table!"

"You—?"

Chase's hair is once again rumpled and there are still circles under his eyes. But he looks great, anyway, in his T-shirt and light-brown Carhartts, which seem to be his work uniform. "You made a table?"

"Come see," she says, tugging his hand.

He shoots me a confused look but follows her into the kitchen, where comprehension dawns. He narrows his eyes at me. I shrug innocently.

We've made him dinner—a steak salad with loads of marinated, grilled sirloin, and little bits of those crispy fried noodles, and plenty of chopped veggies. The steak salad is served on a gorgeous (new) serving platter, and next to it there's a (new) basket, lined with a (new) cloth napkin, full of fresh crusty bread. There's a covered butter tray (new) and a sweet little blunt butter knife (new). There are (new) candles burning in their holders (new) in the center of the table, and each place is set with a (new) cloth placemat, a matching napkin, and a full table setting. I've poured us drinks in wine-glasses (new).

"Daddy, doesn't it look beautiful?"

Out of the mouth of babes.

"It does, honey. It's so beautiful. You did an amazing job. Did you and Liv do all this?"

He says my name like it's a dirty word, and I have to swallow my giggles.

"We went shopping," she says proudly. "We went shopping and we got all the things. I picked the best ones. And then we got the food at the grocery store and we cooked it and we set the table."

"Sit down," I tell him.

He glares at me, but sits, and I serve him steak and salad and bread.

"Is this going on my tab?" he asks.

I smirk in his direction. "Yup."

"Figures," he says, but he doesn't fight me, so he can't be too mad.

I have to hide another smile, as Katie beams at him from behind her plate, eating bread and the noodles and raw veggies out of her salad and, after I cut it into pieces for her, small bits of steak.

"It's all really for Katie," I say, and you should see the dirty look he gives me then.

"Not fair," he mutters, and of course it isn't, and I won't make a habit of it. But Katie's still smiling and I catch the corner of his mouth tipping, the tiniest bit.

7

CHASE

It's pretty much impossible to be angry with Liv, which annoys the shit out of me.

I mean, she's completely messing with me—beautifying my kitchen when I'm not around to defend myself—and she set it up so there's no way I can possibly object without hurting Katie's feelings or acting like an ogre.

On top of that, they both look so happy.

When Celia was here, Katie never looked this happy. I mean, she wasn't outright miserable and crying, but sometimes I thought that was just because Celia had succeeded in placating her with sweets or numbing her out with TV or a movie. At best, she seemed subdued.

But today she's like a little bird, twittery and bright, all smiles, chirpily telling me what she and Liv did, how they went to all these stores and Liv let her choose everything—the placemats, the napkins, the candles. How Liv let her swipe the credit card in the machine and push the cart, how they went to the grocery store and then Liv pushed a chair up to the counter so Katie could help with the cooking, how Liv let Katie set the whole table all by herself because she's a big girl.

And Liv is so damn pleased with herself, like the cat that swallowed the canary. It looks good on her, too. She has this secret smile, a slight soft curve to her lips. Her cheeks glow pink with satisfaction. She's wearing her hair straight today, a long fall of glossy copper.

God, Liv is pretty.

I mean, that's not news to anyone. I've known it since I first walked into Rodro's. Well, shortly after that, when I was done shrieking like the too-stupid-to-live heroine of a horror flick. She's gorgeous, I thought, and then—it was like a body blow—she reminds me of Thea. Not Liv's sweetly rounded face or her runaway curves or the hair like a new penny, but —just the way she was. The way I felt when I saw her, instantly awed and then bristly because of it. Like Thea, she was so put together, so polished—like a stone you pick up on the beach and run your fingers over and over.

Too perfect.

Out of my league.

I was weirdly relieved when Liv said that Camilla had already cockblocked me by telling Liv I was undateable. It wasn't completely unfair. I am a terrible long-term prospect. Good for a good time, but not for a lifetime.

I think if Camilla hadn't cockblocked me, I might have tried something with Liv, and then we would have been over and done. But instead, she's basically my best friend—and an important person in Katie's life.

I actually tried to explain that to my friends today, and failed. I had lunch with Brooks, and two other friends who we often meet up with. Brooks had some Mariners tickets he'd won, and when I told the guys I'd promised Liv I'd be at dinner with her and Katie, they started giving me shit. It's *When Harry Met Sally* syndrome: I swear that movie ruined every last chance for straight men and women to be friends. Well, screw them. Liv and I have proved them wrong, and we'll keep on proving them wrong till she leaves for Colorado.

"Daddy, we got your favorite kind of cake," Katie says.

Nope, can't stay annoyed with either of them.

Liv and Katie clear the table and bring the carrot cake to the table. Liv lets Katie slice it and then helps her tip the slices onto dessert plates. I already owned those plates, because my parents gave me more or less a full set of dishes when I graduated from college. I think they were figuring that I was such a fuck-up that there was absolutely no chance I would ever stumble into marriage and a wedding registry. My mother might actually have been worried that I wouldn't eat at all if they didn't stock my cabinets.

"Daddy, will you play princesses and fairies with me when you're done with your cake?" Katie asks, bouncing up and down in her chair.

Liv raises her eyebrows, and the corner of her mouth quirks.

I glare at her. She knows.

I am not afraid of anything. I swear. I can smash or capture, your choice, those half-dollar-sized hairy-legged spiders. If necessary for the protection of the smaller, weaker, or meeker, I will fight (with fists or words) any person, male or female. I can MacGyver my way through pretty much any survival scenario outdoors with only things I can carry in my pockets (it's helpful if one of them is a paper clip). In the middle of the night, if something makes a noise, I will leap out of bed to go investigate, hoping it's an intruder in need of being taught a lesson.

But Katie's make-believe games terrify me.

I make the mistake of glancing toward Liv again. She gives me a look that if I didn't know better, I would say is a smirk.

"If Liv doesn't need me to help with the dishes?" I say weakly.

"I've got it totally under control," Liv says, biting her lip in what I'm pretty sure is an effort not to laugh at me. "You guys go knock yourselves out. I'll be there in a few."

"C'mon, Daddy!" Katie calls, as she heads for the living room. "I'll get your costume!"

"I suck at princesses and fairies," I whisper.

Liv grins.

"Man up."

8

LIV

When the kitchen is clean, I step into the living room, where I discover Chase wearing a pink tutu and a green straw hat and talking in a high-pitched voice.

"Well, Elsa, where should we go on our adventure?"

Aw. He really is such a good dad.

Chase hasn't noticed me yet, so I draw back against the stairwell and pull my phone out to photograph him in all his glory.

The click of the fake shutter draws Chase's eyes away from Katie—who's wearing an Elsa dress—toward me.

He lunges.

I pocket the phone, laughing like a fiend, ducking out of reach. "Best daddy ever!"

"Just for that, you need to wear a costume, too," Chase says, eyes narrowed. "Katie, who's Liv going to be?"

"Who's your daddy dressed as?" I ask Katie.

"Princess Daddy."

"Princess Daddy," I repeat. "Oh, my. I've got my Facebook caption, then."

Chase glares.

"Not good for the outdoorsy-guy image?"

He gives me the finger outside of Katie's line of sight.

Katie gestures at me to crouch down, and she begins draping me with green fabric that I think was once a Peter Pan costume. "Am I Peter Pan?"

"You're a frog. Hop."

"Wait, what?"

"You're a frog," Katie says patiently. "A really, really, really ugly frog. Hop."

I sneak a glance at Chase's face.

He's trying not to laugh. I raise my eyebrows. He shrugs. "Woman up," he murmurs.

I glare at him.

I crouch and address Katie face to face. "Maybe I could be something else. Like a queen?"

Chase muffles laughter in the crook of his arm.

"No," Katie says, Cupid's-bow mouth set firm. "You're the frog. Hop."

"You could be the frog," I tell Katie. "Don't you want to be the frog?"

"I'm Elsa."

Chase coughs. "We're supposed to be encouraging her to use her imagination, not cramping it. She says I'm the princess and you're the frog. So hop."

I glare, hard, at him, and he smirks back.

"How does Elsa fit into this story?" I ask Katie, trying to buy time.

"After the princess kisses the frog and he turns into a

prince, Elsa builds a magic ice castle for the princess and the prince to live in happily ever after."

"Not all frogs turn into princes when you kiss them," I can't help saying. "And not all stories end with happily ever after."

"Now you're crushing her innocent dreams," Chase murmurs so only I can hear him. I elbow him.

"This one does," says Katie, undaunted.

Even though I've clearly lost this particular battle, I silently cheer for Katie's ability to stand up for herself. And I admit defeat. I hop to the lily pad (pillow) by the stream (where the rug meets the floor). The princess is strolling through the forest.

Actually, the princess is prancing through the forest, clutching what appears to be an invisible parasol.

"I thought you sucked at princess and frogs," I say, sotto voce, when he prances my way. "I feel like I've been hustled."

"Just trying to keep standards high, Ugly Frog."

Snarling, I pull out my phone to video Princess Daddy.

Katie snatches it away and sets it on the coffee table, out of my reach. "Frogs don't have phones."

"I need my phone to video your father!"

"Frogs can't talk," Chase says gleefully.

I dart a dark look his way. "Please," I beg Katie. "The world needs to see this."

"Frogs can't talk," Katie echoes.

Chase is laughing so hard it's impeding his prancing. I clamp my lips shut to hide my own smile.

"You see the frog, Princess Daddy," Katie instructs. "You look down and see him sitting on a lily pad.

"The princess looks down at the frog and the frog looks

up at the princess," Katie intones. "And even though the frog is really, really ugly—"

Chase snickers. I stick my tongue out at him.

"Is that why you didn't want to be the frog?" I ask Katie. "Because he's ugly? Because beauty is only skin deep, you know. I'm full of inner beauty."

I felt the need to get that point in there. I give Chase a *so there* look, and he gives me a *so what* look back.

"Yeah. Elsa is beautiful. The frog is ugly."

"But once I'm a prince I'll be really handsome, right?"

"No. You'll still be really ugly. Like the Beast. And then we'll have to figure out how to lift the other spell on you. The ugly spell. That's why we need the ice castle."

This is a very fractured fairy tale. And I am definitely getting the short end of the narrative stick.

"But Princess Daddy will be beautiful the whole time?"

"Yup. And even though the frog is really, really ugly, Princess Daddy can see his inner beauty. You have to look at each other!" she shouts. "You have to fall madly in love!"

I challenge anyone to disobey a determined five-year-old whose mom has recently passed away. Chase and I do what anyone would do in this situation. We look at each other. And pretend to lock eyes and fall madly in love.

Chase's eyes, as I've mentioned, are beautiful, flecked with color. And full, at the moment, of undisguised glee. But as we stare at each other, something shifts. His eyes get serious. And dark. And my breath hitches in my chest.

Chase's gaze falls to my mouth, and I swear, we are leaning in, closer, closer.

Then, suddenly, as my heart pounds wildly in my chest, Chase draws away.

"Was that good?" Chase demands of Katie.

Oh. Right.

I make a mental note and underline it ten times, until my imaginary pen rips through my imaginary paper.

Chase is not safe for women.

Chase is not safe for me.

9

CHASE

The next morning, I'm in the car, messing with the sound system, when I realize I don't have my phone on me.

I've been off my game all morning, and I blame Katie's Princess Daddy make-believe. What *was* that, anyway? One minute I was obeying Katie's goofy commandment to pretend to fall in love with Liv, and the next I was staring into Liv's beautiful green eyes, feeling like I'd actually stumbled under some kind of spell. The princess, frozen in place by the frog's gaze.

Then Liv's breath hitched, her chest rising abruptly, and my eyes instinctively needed to see more. To see her pretty tits moving under her tight t-shirt. Except my own gaze got caught on the way down, snagged on the soft curve of her lower lip.

It would feel so fucking good to suck on that sweet flesh and lift a hand to shape and cup her.

I could do it.

She was leaving. It wasn't like I could destroy our friendship now. She'd made it clear our friendship wouldn't outlast our geographical proximity.

Only the fact that Katie was standing right there kept me from lowering my mouth to Liv's and helping myself to all that gorgeous softness.

So yeah. Off my game this morning.

I head back inside. Katie is sitting at the kitchen table, swinging her feet as she works on some kind of craft project that involves teeny tiny gems and a paint-by-number scenario.

"Did Liv give you that?" I ask her.

"Uh-huh!" she says, beaming at me.

Such an improvement over non-stop *Frozen*.

"I forgot my phone, so I just came back to look for it."

"Okay," she says with a shrug.

Katie apparently doesn't mind me leaving for work at all when Liv's here. Maybe I can judge whether a nanny is any good by how the departures go. Filed away.

I search all over the kitchen and living room for my phone. Then I remember: I left it in the bathroom, blue-toothed into the waterproof speaker. I take the stairs two at a time and jog down the hall to the bathroom. The door's partially open, so I assume Liv's in her room and swing it open further, only to be confronted with:

Liv, completely naked, applying deodorant, singing quietly to herself in the mirror, swaying her booty in a flirty little dance that no one was ever meant to see.

Her long, pale, satiny back, the flare from her waist to the generous curve of her hips and ass. Creamy and smooth. A little jiggle as she moves—jiggle that makes my mouth water and my hands itch.

A strangled noise escapes my throat.

She drops the deodorant and turns, which is the worst thing she could possibly have done, because now she is facing me, naked, and I can't look away, not from the sight of her perfect pink-tipped breasts, topped with freckles, or the small, neat triangle of bright red hair. I want to drop to my knees and put my mouth there—

She shrieks and grabs for a towel, covering all that gorgeousness with worn blue terrycloth.

"Jesus, Chase, what the *fuck!*?"

"I—"

I'm all ready to apologize, when I realize that in fact, I haven't done anything remotely outrageous. "What are you— what—why—why is the door open?!" I demand instead.

She's wrapping herself in the towel like she's trying to put the genie back in the jar, but let me tell you, that fucking genie is not going back in the jar. Any more than my cock will return to its pre-view state any time in the next few minutes.

She bites her lip. The one I still want to suck on. "I wanted to be able to hear Katie if she needed me," she says.

"Oh," I say, chastened. "Fair enough." And then I remember that I still haven't explained myself. "Phone," I say lamely, pointing to the counter behind her. "I forgot it."

I'm still having some trouble with sentences.

One hand tightly gripping the towel—which, I might point out, still leaves a lot of soft skin exposed—she reaches for the phone and holds it out gingerly, like it might explode.

No, that would be me.

I take the phone and turn to go. I need to get out of here. The ideal place for me to go would be someplace quiet and private where I could spend a few minutes grappling with the steel rod behind my zipper and the picture of Liv in my head, but I'm really late for work now, and I have to run.

"Chase," she calls, as I stride toward the stairs.

I turn back.

"Can we forget this ever happened?" she says, gesturing with her free hand in the general direction of her terry-wrapped body. That towel might as well be transparent, because I can still see the image of her burned onto the back of my brain.

"Absolutely," I say, before running down the stairs, out of the house, and to my car.

I'm such a fucking liar.

I am *never* forgetting that happened.

10

CHASE

"And then you divide by the number of innings pitched..."

My Saturday night date, Ava, is explaining to the little boy sitting a couple of seats over how to calculate the ERA stat. His dad tried, but hit a wall, so she took over.

We're at Safeco Field, sitting side by side. It's a blue-sky, sunny summer evening, and, well, I'm a mess.

Ava is great.

She loves sports. When I PM'd her on the online dating site to ask, *Baseball game?* she immediately texted back, *OMG, are you for real? I love baseball. Buy me a hot dog and some Cracker Jacks and I'm all yours.*

That might be two boxes checked, actually: loves sports and eats real food.

Plus, if you count "I'm all yours" as a come-on—which I do, being a guy—you might even be able to check a third box: not shy about sex.

I wrote back, *Sounds like I'm getting the best end of the deal.*

So far, she's lived up to her promise. She's put away two

hot dogs and is midway through her second beer. Her base-ball cred is real: she's actually scoring the game in her program, including every ball and strike. Apparently her dad taught her to do it when she was a kid, and she has a set of binders at home with every game she's ever been to. She told me about the first time she went to a game, Yankees v. Orioles at Yankee Stadium, and what it felt like to walk into the park for the first time—the hush before the crack of the bat, the bright green field suddenly wide open in front of her, the smell of grass and dirt and hot dogs and peanuts and beer.

And she's cute. Long, shiny blond hair pulled back in a high ponytail (sexy and low maintenance), a killer tan, big blue eyes, and a great bod. Check, check, check, and check.

Plus—she likes kids, or at least it seems like she must, because who else would explain baseball to a little boy she doesn't even know?

She rises out of her seat, cheering wildly with the rest of the fans as our batter hits a near-home-run ball that drops into the right-field corner.

Perfect, right? So why am I such a mess? I should be ecstatic.

It's because I can't stop thinking of Liv.

Liv, playing the frog, gazing faux-longingly into my eyes.

Liv, from behind, a perfect hourglass of lickability.

Liv, spinning to face me, breasts bouncing from the abrupt movement, two handfuls my palms are still itching to cup.

I can feel those pretty nipples against my palms, rising to meet my touch.

"I'm going to get a beer," Ava says. "Do you want me to get you one?"

I snap back to the present, pissed at myself. I've almost forgotten her, and it's a point of pride that I never do that, never think about another woman when I'm with one. I'm here, with Ava, and that's where my mind should be.

If I didn't think I could do this like a man, I should have canceled the date.

I probably should have canceled the date.

But I'm here now, and I'm going to try my hardest not to be a fuckboy.

"No way. I'll get 'em. You stay here and hold down the fort."

"Aw. That's so incredibly sweet."

"Hey," I say lightly. "What kind of asshole makes you get your own beer on a first date at a baseball game?"

"Guess I've dated all the wrong guys," she teases, with a suggestive little smile.

The problem is, it makes me think about the secret smile Liv wore when she and Katie unveiled the table they'd set for me. It wasn't about sex, but it was sexy nonetheless.

I've spent so long putting Liv in a not-like-that category, and now I can't keep her there.

I trudge up the stadium steps and find my way along the mezzanine to one of the places that sells decent microbrews. The lines are epic. Seventh-inning-stretch beer is a hard-won prize.

My phone buzzes. A text from Liv. Actually, a whole string of them. How'd I miss them?

Girls' night out!

There's a photo attached, a selfie of her and Katie sitting at the local pizzeria, grinning from ear to ear. Katie's hair is in two curly pigtails and looks adorable. The photo is taken slightly downward, right into the lush curves of Liv's cleavage.

My mouth goes dry.

The next photo is them eating ice cream, each of them clutching a cone.

I get this instant, hot flash of an image: Liv's tongue sweeping out to lick the drips of the ice cream at the seam where cream meets crunch.

C'mon, man!

It's because I'm overdue, right? Which is why I'm out on this date, because no man is an island, and even dads have to get laid from time to time or they start having unwanted fantasies about their temporary nannies/best friends.

The last text says *Reading with Katie. Next up: Chick flick on the couch.* The photo is the two of them propped together on Katie's pillows with *The Araboolies of Liberty Street* in their laps. They are really cute sitting side by side like that. And Katie looks—

She looks so freaking happy.

This is the first time she's been happy like this for days at a time since Thea died.

But it's temporary.

Liv is leaving.

The future is sitting in a seat in the stadium, waiting for her beer.

"Can I help you?" A gruff voice breaks into my musings.

I've reached the front of the concession line, and I stow my phone so I can place my drink order and carry the beers. For good measure, I buy my perfect date a hot pretzel and a bag of M&M's. A girl who appreciates a ballpark hot dog and a box of Cracker Jacks is obviously all about the best things in life.

I carry the beers and snacks back to our seats, where the bottom of the seventh is nearly over, thanks to the hapless A's, and she rewards my efforts with a big smile. "I looove M&M's!" she says.

I sit next to her and she offers me some M&M's.

Oh, wait. I never replied to Liv's text. I reach for my phone—

Nope. Nope, nope, nope. One of my top ten rules of dating—actually, one of my top ten rules for being a decent human being—is that when you're hanging out with someone, you give that person your undivided attention. You don't futz with your email or answer texts or check in to make sure you haven't missed breaking news or your boss's latest whim.

Or, you know, think about your best friend's tongue in totally illicit ways.

I let my hand drop back to my side, but it's like an itch, those texts. I want to text back, *What, you'll slum it and eat pizza for Katie, but not for me?* Or something equally dorky. Just some dumb joke to let Liv know I'm thinking of her—

Everyone around me soars to their feet—something epic has happened and I wasn't paying any attention. Two-run homer. While everyone's riveted by the action on the field, I find myself sliding the phone a little ways out of my pocket, then jamming it back in, like I'm a junkie and it's my fix. I read this study somewhere that having your phone in front of you facedown on the table while you're trying to accomplish a task is more distracting than listening to music. Irritated with my weakness, I vow to give Ava my undivided attention for the rest of the game.

The Mariners win it.

I follow Ava out of the stadium, the two of us swept along on the wave of the exiting crowd.

On the way back to the car, with the baseball game no longer holding our attention, we fall back on small talk. She asks me to tell her about Mike's Mountainwear, and once I've done that, I ask her to tell me about her big family—five girls! —which turns into a funny but meandering analysis of her relationship with each of her sisters.

She's smart. And witty. And—did I mention cute? If we were having this conversation at a cocktail party, I'd probably be trying to figure out how to get her to leave the party with me.

But when I pull up in front of her apartment and she says, "Hey. You want to come in for a drink or something?" I already know I'm not going to say *I'd love that*.

"Thanks," I say. "I had a really good time. But, um—"

Honestly? I don't even know how the sentence ends.

She looks at me with confusion all over her face, which is totally fair. She is a beautiful woman with a terrific body, and I don't imagine there are many guys who have ever hesitated this long over the question of whether they want to be alone with her in her apartment.

"Thanks, but I should get home. Early morning tomorrow."

Her smile falls.

"Okay," she says. "Well, um—call me?"

I'm about to say I will. But then something stops me. Instead I say, "You know, I had a really good time, but I don't think it's going to happen."

"Oh," she says. Sadly. So sadly I want to tell her I'm making a mistake—

"I know this is the worst fucking cliché? But it's not you."

That makes her scrunch up her face.

"I know," I say. "But in this case, it's actually true. I think I'm—not—over someone."

Her expression softens a bit. "That makes a lot of sense," she says.

She gets out of the car and waves goodbye and I pull away from the curb. Headed home.

Which—if we're being honest with ourselves—is where I've wanted to be all evening.

11

LIV

When Chase comes home, one of the women in the movie, Simone, has been diagnosed with pancreatic cancer. Tears are pouring down my face. I'm crying so hard, I almost don't hear the door. This group of friends, they have such an awful shared history, but they've always been there for each other, and Simone is such a gentle person, like, I don't know, Beth in *Little Women*. She doesn't deserve this. It's so unfair.

I pause the movie, grab a wad of tissues from the box on the coffee table, and scrub the tears away.

Chase comes into the living room.

"Oh, wow," he says, taking in my tear-ravaged face. "Wait. No, don't tell me. Someone dies?"

I punch him in the shoulder.

"Ow." He plops down on the couch beside me. He looks good. Worn jeans, thin where his thighs strain the denim, and a gray Mariners T-shirt with navy trim, including bands that stretch over his biceps. He tosses his baseball cap on the coffee table. His hair, of course, is a total, gorgeous mess.

I really need things to get back to normal with Chase. It was bad enough that I had kissing thoughts about him while playing make-believe. But then he saw me naked, and ever since then, I've had trouble getting the look on his face out of my head.

Those whiskey eyes, dark with male admiration. But not just appreciation.

Need.

Hunger.

I felt that look—before he locked it down and smoothed his expression out—settle, hot and liquid, between my legs.

I need this place to stay, the money, and Chase's friendship too much to fuck it up by letting him play one-night-and-only-one-night with me.

So I keep my voice light when I ask, "Shitty date?"

He gives me a weird look. "It was fine."

"It's only midnight."

"I can get a lot done in a short time."

It shouldn't, but that makes me laugh. I don't doubt it. "So —on a scale of, I don't know, 'would rather have watched a movie' to 'planning marriage proposal'?"

"Um, I don't know; it was fine."

Chase is never cagey with me. Or at least not in this way. I raise my eyebrows. "I might need a little more than that."

"Whatever," he says irritably. "She was cute. Blond. Loves sports. Scored the game, explained ERA to the kid next to us—"

I feel an unfamiliar twinge. Like—jealousy? Because some cute blond girl knows stuff about baseball?

Surely not.

"—likes stadium food. Seems really easygoing. Loves

camping, loves playing sports, too—she plays pickup basket-ball and Ultimate Frisbee—"

He's ticking off the items on his perfect-woman checklist, one by one.

I roll my eyes. "She's perfect, but . . .?" I draw the last word out. "Without getting into gory details, what happened?"

"I just—I don't know, whatever."

"It was just, whatever?" I ask incredulously. "What does that even mean? Did you kiss her?"

He shakes his head.

I stare at him, agog.

"She was cute, loves sports, loves camping, likes crappy stadium food—"

"I didn't say 'crappy,'" he mutters.

"Likes *stadium* food... But you didn't kiss her. Did you go for it and she rejected you?"

He crosses his arms and glares at me. "No. She invited me up."

"And you turned her *down*?"

Now he won't look at me. "I don't know." He shrugs. "She wasn't all that, you know?"

"Are you going to see her again?"

He sighs. "Probably not."

"Chase? We've been friends for a long time, right?"

"Yeah."

"So can I ask you kind of a personal question?"

"No," he says.

"I'm going to ask anyway."

"I knew you would."

"What do you want from them? The women you go out with?"

His eyes widen.

"Because, honestly? It seems like the more you like them, the less likely you are to see them twice."

"Yeah?" He tilts his head, considering. Then he shrugs again. "You may be on to something."

"And tonight kind of convinced me. Because you actually went out with the perfect woman, and where are you? Not boning her. Not cuddling in her bed. Hanging with me."

He's giving me a weird look now. "I like hanging with you."

"I guess that's sort of my point. You like hanging with me because I'm safe and you know there's no way in hell I'll stop being safe. But if there's a woman you actually like and are attracted to? You run."

He opens his mouth, then shuts it again.

Shit. I've gone too far.

"You—might be right."

Okay, that was so not the response I was expecting. I was expecting him to get mad or say something else, but he looks thoughtful. He pushes himself to his feet and says, "I'm going to get myself a beer. Switch to your iPad, and we'll have an official consolation party."

Okay then. Conversation over.

He goes into the kitchen and comes back with a beer and his iPad. He dims the light and plops down on the couch next to me. Fiddles around with the Netflix app.

"What're you watching?"

"*The Fate of the Furious*. The eighth Fast and Furious movie."

"Of course you are," I sigh.

"At least my movie doesn't deplete the rain forest by using up all the tissues in the house."

I stick my tongue out at him and pull the tissue box closer.

We watch for a while side by side.

I think about the fact that sometimes I go to the movies with Eve. We sit together and share popcorn and Junior Mints. We watch the same movie. We cry at the same time.

That's the gold standard, right?

I guess all I'm saying is that I've never understood why sitting side by side in Chase's living room with two different movies and two different drinks should feel so—I don't know...

Cozy.

Homey.

Right.

12

CHASE

"Holy shit."

Liv turns from where she is straightening a framed photo on the wall in her room. "I'm going to take that as a compliment," she says dryly.

It's Sunday afternoon. I came upstairs because I heard hammering, and when you hear hammering in your house, it's usually a good idea to check it out.

Somehow, Liv has turned my dull-ass guest room into something out of a magazine. A couple of hours ago it was a big blank—white walls, drab carpet, a bed made up with camp-style blankets and a lone pillow, some stacked milk crates, and a shabby dresser.

She has transformed it into a beach cottage, all light and airy. The bed is neatly made up with blue-and-white bedding. The windows are covered with sheer white curtains and framed with a cobalt-blue scarf. She has draped white fabric over the milk crates and dresser and arranged knick-knacks on top—including a mason jar full of vivid sea glass. As I watch, she hangs a photo of a beach, beside two others.

"You did this for *two weeks*?" I demand.

She nods. "Ninety-two," she says.

"What?"

"You were going to ask. How much I spent. Ninety-two dollars."

"I wasn't going to ask, but—how the hell did you do all this for ninety-two dollars?"

She shows me, item by item. The bedding came first, and she chose it because it was on sale at Target. Then she filled in at Goodwill. The photos are pages cut from a travel magazine and framed in the cheapest matching frames she could lay her hands on.

"If I had more time, or a bigger budget, I could have done something more creative than a beach cottage theme."

"It seems pretty creative to me."

"I mean, a beach cottage design is kind of a cliché at this point. But I also knew it would be relatively easy to do. And I'm not staying long, so I didn't want to get too complicated."

"Then—then why? Why do it at all?"

For a moment I think she's not going to answer. Then she says, "It's something I learned from a foster sister, in my—" She counts off on her fingers. "—fourth foster home. She called it carrying her shell on her back. They can keep moving you around, and there are so many things you can't take with you, but you can make every place your own, no matter how short a time you're there. It helps."

I think that's more than Liv has ever said before about growing up in foster care. She plays her cards close to her chest when it comes to that topic.

I wonder what it would feel like to have moved around as much as she has. To never have one place feel like home.

I don't think I'd like it.

"Are you still close to your foster sister?"

She shakes her head. "She didn't want to stay in touch. She said it wasn't a good idea. Better to make a clean break and move on."

That kind of hurts my heart. And also makes me understand something about Liv that I've never gotten before. "That's why you think that, too."

"I think it because it's true," she says tightly.

I tilt my head, taking in her grumpy frown.

"Hey, Liv? How can I make myself eligible to stay your friend when you go to Golden?"

She scrunches up her forehead. "Would you really want that?"

"I mean, we could FaceTime and watch separate movies."

"It wouldn't be the same."

A few days ago, I would probably have agreed with her. But the thought of her disappearing to Golden without a trace doesn't sit as well with me today.

"At least can you keep in touch with Katie?"

She thinks about that. "I could do that."

She returns to straightening the beach photo. I think we're done—and I don't want to be done. I want to know more about the inner workings of Liv.

"How old were you when you went into foster care?"

"My mom died when I was seven."

My chest aches. "Not so different from Katie."

She smiles, but there's tightness to it.

"Is it hard for you, with Katie, because of that?"

She shakes her head. "I don't think of it that way. I think it helps me understand what Katie is going through. It helps me to help her."

I know that's not the whole story. Under all that bravado there must still be a scared little girl. I feel a special kind of sympathy for the younger Liv. And a lot of admiration for the woman she's become.

Some of what I'm feeling must show on my face, because she says, "When people hear I lived in foster homes, their minds always go to the worst place. But for me, it wasn't so bad. They were full of well-meaning adults who wanted to help. The only hard part was, I never got to stay. I'd start to feel like I'd settled in, and then something would happen. Another child would need the spot more than I did. A foster mom had a breakdown, a foster brother abused a sister, a foster dad got busted for possession. So that's why I loved the idea so much of carrying my house around with me like a shell."

I gesture to the room around us. "When you go to Golden, you'll do this all over again?"

She nods. "And after that, wherever I go next."

"Are you—looking forward to going to Golden?"

I'm not sure why I'm asking, or what I want her to say.

"I am. I get twitchy if I stay in a place too long. Claustrophobic. Literally, I start to itch. I can't concentrate."

"I have that. I mean, not for living in a place too long, but . . ."

She tilts her head.

"As a kid, I wanted to be outside all the time. Fishing or hunting or camping with my uncle or if I couldn't do that, tromping around the woods, hiking, foraging, snowshoeing, skiing—anything that would get me outside. Outside, I was—

I don't know. Real. Alive. Inside, I was—like you're saying. Trapped."

It was the subject of so many fights between me and my parents. Weekends, I wanted nothing more than to be in the woods with my uncle, but they insisted I stay home and study. They hired tutors for me. They forced me to take piano lessons. They were constantly trying to make me the son they wanted instead of the one I was.

Liv is watching me sympathetically. "That's why the outerwear store is so perfect for you, right?"

I hesitate. "I guess."

Her brows draw together. "What is it?"

"I worked on the business plan this morning."

"Chase! That's terrific!" She beams.

"I found a site with a template, and I'm using that. I have no idea if I'm doing it right—"

"You're doing great."

That's all she says. But she says it quietly. Simply. And it helps. Her faith in me helps.

We sit for a while, not talking. It reminds me of watching the movies side by side, like we're both thinking about what's in our heads, together, but separately.

Her phone buzzes on the nightstand and she reaches for it.

"Chase. Could you interview a potential nanny on Monday, August twenty-eighth?"

"Sure."

"It's only three days before I leave—but I'm pretty darn sure you're going to want to hire her. She's really good. I know I said that about Celia—"

"That was a fluke. I trust your judgment."

The phone buzzes again and she looks down. "Eight p.m.?"

"Whatever works."

She texts something. "Okay. Eight on August twenty-eighth."

"Remind me to put it in my calendar, because there's no way I'll remember if I don't."

Mention of the word calendar reminds me: "Remember I told you my parents are coming tomorrow night on their way back from a trip? You, um, want to eat with us? If you haven't already made plans?"

Her eyebrows go up. "Do you want me to be there?"

I love my parents; I really do. But sometimes it's easier with them if it's a little more . . . casual. And having Liv and Katie both there would definitely take some of the focus off the old, um, issues between us.

I nod. And that's all it takes. She says, "I'll be there. It'll be cool to meet your parents."

"I don't think cool is the word you're looking for."

"It will be educational."

That makes me smile.

She tilts her head. "I could make spaghetti bolognese and garlic bread and salad. Katie would like that, too."

"Put me in charge of the garlic bread and the salad."

She raises her eyebrows.

"I'm not totally helpless in the kitchen."

"Deal," she says. "Also—if you want help with the business plan thing—I don't know anything, but two heads are better than one, right?"

"I'm around tonight. Nothing going on."

I have to admit, the idea of spending an evening kicking

back on the couch next to Liv, talking about the store, sounds pretty fucking awesome.

"Oh. Um. I can't tonight. I have a date."

"Oh." Damn, that's right; she'd mentioned that. "First date?" I ask, trying to recover my equilibrium. Because of course she's not going to spend her night off helping me write a business plan. Duh.

"We've been out twice. His name is Kieran."

Oh, so not just a date. A *third* date.

Not that it should matter whether it's a first, second, third, or twentieth date. Or whether we're talking awkward small talk or the horizontal mambo. But I find myself asking, "Have you told me about this guy?"

"He's . . ."

She hesitates, and something in my chest contracts. She has a distant look on her face. As if thinking about how to describe him has made her a little dreamy.

I don't like it.

I don't want Liv getting dreamy about this guy, whoever he is.

And yeah, Chase? What are you going to do about it?

"He took me to Canlis on our first date."

"Now that's just showing off. He went for the low-hanging fruit, seduction-wise—candlelight, fancy food. It doesn't mean he's your type." I keep my voice light, but let's face it, I mean what I'm saying. She can't fall for a snow job like that, can she?

"He is, though," she says, quietly. "He loves gourmet food, likes live music and art museums, and I saw his apartment— it's very classily decorated."

She saw his apartment?

She must hear what she's said at the same minute I do, because she blushes. "Nothing happened. We hung out and then he kissed me good night." She blushes even more fiercely, the color spreading to the tips of her ears.

"You don't need my permission," I say testily. Because, damn, I like the look of that blush on her, but I hate the idea that this other guy has put it there.

"I wasn't asking for it," she says simply. Not defensively at all.

"Does he know you're moving to Golden?"

"Yeah."

"And?"

"Well, I mean, he's not psyched about it. But his company has an office in Golden, so he'll be in town from time to time."

"Wait," I say. "Wait. He's going to visit you?"

"I mean, I doubt he will. I doubt I'll want him to. But it's come up."

"He gets to fly out, but we can't watch movies on FaceTime?"

She stares at me, like I've lost my mind, which maybe I have.

"If you want to watch movies on FaceTime, we can," she says, a touch irritably.

"Whatever. I don't care if we watch movies or not. I'll find someone else to watch movies with. Katie and I will watch movies together."

There is a small furrow in her forehead, between her eyebrows.

I turn away so she can't see the expression on my face, which is—honestly, I don't know. Hurt, I think, although why the hell I'd be hurt that she's going to let Kieran fly out to Golden and visit her, I don't know.

"Chase," she says.

"Don't worry about it." I manage a slightly more convincing tone this time. I head for the door, although I can still feel her staring at me, her puzzlement a thread between us. "I'll let you get back to beautifying the world."

Her gaze follows me all the way out.

13

LIV

When I get home from my date, I park my car outside Chase's house and quietly let myself in.

Chase is sprawled on the couch in a pair of cutoff shorts and a T-shirt, his arm behind his head. Thoroughly relaxed.

He surveys me, a question on his face.

"What?"

"You don't look very 'third date.'"

"What's that supposed to mean?"

"You know, third date. The sex date? You don't look like you've had amazing sex."

I roll my eyes. "There's no such thing as that look."

"There is." He looks me up and down appraisingly, and I blush—not because I've done anything to blush about, but because the appraisal heats my body. Or maybe it's that he's seen me naked. Is he thinking about that?

Why am I thinking about that?

"Nope, you don't have the sex look. So, bad date?"

He's so unbelievably cocky and irritating sometimes. An

internal imp—or maybe an instinct for self-preservation—makes me say, "It was really fun."

Chase's expression doesn't change. Which isn't so surprising, but it still irks me.

"Where'd you go?" he asks.

"We went to see a play. *Six Doors*. Based on this novel that was super-popular a couple of years ago."

"Ah, you went to the thea-tah," he mocks airily, in a pretty damn good upper-crust British accent.

"It was really good." That's not a lie. It was a great play. In fact, there was nothing wrong with the choice of venues, the play itself, the dinner afterward, or Kieran. But there was something wrong with my head.

It kept leaping ahead to the part of the evening where I would debrief the date with Chase. Then I'd catch myself and remind myself that I was with Kieran. Kieran. I was supposed to be enjoying my time with him, not cataloguing what I'd say about him to another guy, later.

"I'm sure it was delightful," Chase says "Every girl loves the thea-tah. And din-nah afterwards, right, dahling?"

I smile at that. "Sushi."

"Sushi. Of course. Takeout?"

I wince. "Yes."

"At his place?"

Yes, but the last thing I want to do is talk with Chase about what happened at Kieran's place. For so many reasons.

"None of your business." I desperately hope that ends this thread of questioning.

"Oho! She got action, ladies and gentlemen!"

I flinch, internally. I shrug, and hope my face doesn't give me away.

"Was it all you wanted and more?"

"It was—"

I look up and see his face. Corner-to-corner smirk. Somehow, I have no idea how, he knows it wasn't a success.

For a moment, I teeter between hating him for mocking me and loving him for knowing, without my having to say it, that the date was a disappointment.

"I bet Kieran's one and only flaw is that he's a terrible kisser."

Now I want to kill him.

Because he's smug. And smirking. And because, of course, he's right.

While Kieran is not a terrible kisser, he's not a great one, either.

Or maybe we didn't have the right kissing chemistry. I'm not sure. All I know is that during our two make-out sessions, I was unable to stop noticing everything. I mean, everything. I was hyper-aware of what was wrong with with Kieran's kissing—teeth clashing, tongue poking, that weird sipping thing he was doing.

After a while, I had to tell Kieran the truth.

This, um, isn't working for me.

Tell me what I can do to make it good for you.

I winced.

Oh. You mean, really not working.

As breakups go, it was bloodless. He was a good sport about it. Some woman will win the prize when she finds him.

Just not me.

Chase is staring at me like he can see my thoughts, which is a disconcerting idea. "What?" I demand.

"Why do you go out with these guys you aren't even really into?"

I'm about to snap back at him, but let's face it, I said something pretty similar to him last night.

"Seriously, Liv, the only difference between me and you is that you string the guys along for a couple of weeks or months before you bail out."

Oh, now wait a second. Them's fighting words. "I don't string anyone along."

"You kinda do, though. I mean, you deliberately pick these great-on-paper guys that don't do anything for you."

I know it's crazy, I know I should keep my mouth shut, but he's really pissing me off. I cross my arms. "How do you know Kieran doesn't do it for me?"

He stares at me like this is an absolutely bonkers question. Then he levers himself off the couch, and my mouth goes dry.

My heart starts pounding at the look in his eyes—slow-burning and intense.

I instinctively take a step back. Because—well, a million things. Because if he's about to do what I think he's about to do, it will confuse everything.

"So Kieran 'does it for you,'" Chase says slowly, his eyes never leaving mine.

I'm frozen in place, pinned by the heavy-lidded look. A look even more predatory than the one that flashed across his face when he saw me naked.

He steps closer to me.

"So when he gets close, you feel this?"

His body is not quite touching mine, but it might as well

be, because he's brought every hair to attention, every nerve screaming to life.

"F-f-feel what?" I squeak. Even though I know exactly what he means. He's talking about the heat that's filled up all the available space in the room, all the emptiness in my body. That rich, melting sensation that has invaded me. The sweet swirl low in my belly, pulling me toward him.

He's so close. All I'd have to do is tip my face up and lean in a fraction and we'd be kissing.

That thought sends a surge of heat across my chest and face and makes my legs wobbly.

His eyes on my face flash satisfaction. He saw me blush. "Well?" he demands. "Is this what it feels like?"

I'm frozen. I can't speak.

"Yeah." His smirk is gone. His eyes are dark and hot. "That's what I thought."

He wraps his hands in my hair. I feel the tug not only on my scalp but also in my nipples and between my legs. Despite my best intentions, I make a sound. Pretty sure it qualifies as a whimper.

My breasts tighten and my nipples pinch as the solid planes of his chest collide with me, and my mouth waters at the sharp smell of soap and lemongrass-evergreen-wood-smoke aftershave. And his skin itself. That scent doesn't have a name, only an effect—like the last sigh you breathe out before you relax your body completely in bed, in total surrender.

And yes, that's what I do: I give in, I give myself up. His mouth floats down to mine and settles softly but with total certainty, and I hear his sigh of satisfaction, and then I am lost to his lips, warm and commanding, and his tongue, which strokes into my mouth before I'm aware of opening it.

His hands leave my hair to map my waist and hips, and before I can stop him, curve around to cup my behind and tug me up against him.

Wow.

That is a lot of Chase.

I whimper again.

Which makes him groan.

That's when my body really goes into overdrive.

I wasn't expecting how good it would feel to make Chase lose control.

Too good. Way too good.

I take a step back. And then another. And as I do—as the space between us widens and clarity returns to my fogged brain—I realize that I reacted to that kiss like it was real—when Chase was just trying to prove something about Kieran.

"What do you think you're doing?"

"I—don't—I don't know." He sounds genuinely uncertain.

"Are you just trying to one-up Kieran? To prove some kind of macho point?"

"No. I don't know."

"Well, whatever is it, don't."

His head comes up, and his brows draw together. "I'm right, though, Liv. You have to admit that."

"Right about what?"

"Tell me it didn't feel . . ." He hesitates. "So fucking good."

His words shimmy down my insides, lighting me up. I come so damn close to getting sucked back in—to the heat in his eyes and the magnetic pull coming off his bare skin.

Instead, I say, as calmly as I can, "Chase?"

"Yeah?"

"I'm going upstairs. And this?"

"Yeah?"

"None of this happened."

And I walk away.

14

CHASE

I do what any half-sane man would do in my shoes, I run for the shower.

Cold would be the smart move, but I go for so hot it hurts. Maybe I can scald some sense into myself.

But probably not. Because basically?

I want more.

I didn't mean to kiss her.

I mean, I did and I didn't.

I meant to kiss her. Hell, I couldn't not kiss her.

I just didn't mean to kiss her like that. Under those circumstances.

I got so mad when she started bullshitting me. It made me go crazy, and that's why I said what I said and did what I did, the way I did.

But I should have done it right. Above board.

I should have told her that something was going on in my head. I should have told her how much I wanted her, that I thought we could give those feelings some rein, to see if it would feel as good to kiss and touch and all the rest as it felt to stand near each other.

Answer, by the way: Standing close to Liv feels like sparks trying to burst into flame. Kissing her, pressing my body against hers—feels like being on fire.

As for what it would feel like to lean into that fire, to feel all that soft, satin naked skin against mine—

I groan.

God damn, I want that.

And I'm pretty sure—I'm pretty sure she does, too. Even if she doesn't know it or want to admit it.

I can't have lost my chance. I can't. Because it was too good, and I want more. I want Liv more than I've ever wanted anyone.

The water is raining down over me, scalding and delicious, and my cock is hard from everything that happened and everything I want to happen.

I wrap my fist around myself. I'm hard enough to pound nails.

I want another chance. I want to give her a demo of what it feels like to be kissed so deep and so well that remembering it will make her hot all over again. So hot she can't string five words together.

I want to make her wet and soft and open and full of sighs and whimpers.

I want to pick up where we left off. That's what I want to do.

I stroke myself, imagining. The sweet give of her lower lip, the way she'd press her curves against me, her pretty nipples hardening against my chest and her pubic bone, red curls and all, tipping against my dick.

I imagine getting her so worked up she'd have no choice but to tell me the truth. "I was never into Kieran. I'm into you, Chase. I'm so into you. I need you. Now."

I imagine how it would feel to have her breasts and her ass naked in my palms, handfuls of her as I—

I fist myself, hand rocking down, hips pushing forward, skin taut, sensation boiling up so fucking fast from the base of my spine that I can't hold it back.

This is Liv. My friend Liv.

I don't care. I just care about the images and fantasy sensations that are careening through my head now, one after the other, the way she'd look naked, the way my lips and tongue would slick her pussy, the way I'd suck her nipples hard into my mouth, the way I'd lay her back on my bed and plunge, burying myself in her.

And I'm coming so hard I bite my lip to keep from groaning out loud.

15

LIV

E ve and I meet for breakfast the next morning, Monday, at our favorite diner.

"Hey," I say, plopping down across from her.

"What's wrong?"

"Nothing."

She tilts her head. "Bullshit."

Now that's a good friend, right? "Um. You remember how when I said I was moving in with Chase, you asked if I knew what I was doing?"

Both her eyebrows shoot up. "Yeah."

"And I said, 'Nothing will ever happen between Chase and me. Not in a million years. From a sexual perspective, it's as safe as sleeping on your couch.'"

If possible, her eyebrows go higher. "I do remember that. Very clearly."

"Well, unless there's something you're not telling me about your couch, I was wrong."

She whistles. "I knew it! Holy shit, Liv, what happened?"

I frown at her. "It's nice of you not to say 'I told you so.'"

"A saint would say 'I told you so' in this situation," she says.

Eve, like most people, doesn't believe men and women can be friends. To quote *When Harry Met Sally*, she thinks the sex always gets in the way. Plus, she and Rodro and Camilla have been mystified all along by Chase's and my friendship. If we get along so well, and we're both attractive, what's preventing us from bonking like bunnies?

Not much, apparently.

"What happened?"

The waitress is eyeing our still untouched menus. "We should order first."

"Quit stalling," Eve commands, but we do put our orders in, and then I do my best to give her an accurate accounting of what's gone down. It feels like about ten lifetimes, but it's less than a week.

When I get to the part where Chase says, "So when he gets close, you feel this?" Eve shakes her head in disbelief, and—I think—awed respect for Chase's moves. And why shouldn't she? He did reduce me to jelly in seconds flat.

She's shaking her head again when I finish the story. "How do you know he was trying to prove a point?"

"What else would he have been trying to do?"

She stares long and hard at me, but doesn't contradict.

I say, "I think I should come back to your place."

"You can't do that! First of all, you need the money. But you also can't bail out on Katie and Chase."

"Screw Chase. He kissed me. But you're right about Katie. I can't bail on her." I sigh. "And I need the money."

Eve squints at me. "Even if you didn't, are you sure you'd want to walk away from Chase?"

"What's the alternative?"

"Tell him you didn't mean what you said about it never happening. Tell him it happened and you want it to happen again."

My mouth falls open. "You can't be serious."

"Let me ask you something. Was it good?"

That was the one set of details I left out of my retelling. And I apparently am not going to get away with it.

Eve crows. "The answer is obviously yes. You're blushing."

I turn away. "I am not."

"You are too."

I know she's right; my face is hot enough to power Seattle's grid. The waitress chooses that moment to show up with Eve's French toast and my avocado-and-tomato omelette. I glare at Eve across the table and she smiles sweetly back.

We dig into our food, and I mentally cross my fingers that she's been diverted from her previous line of questioning.

No such luck. "Tell me," Eve demands.

"None of your business!"

"I'm your best friend, right?" she asks. "I at least merit a summary."

I know she's right. As much as I don't want it to have happened, I don't want to lie to myself about it, either. "It was so good. Ridiculously good. Life-changingly good. But there are so many reasons it's a bad idea."

"Name one."

"He's my friend."

"Have I ever told you my Pandora's Box theory of friends and sex? It's not going back in the box, Liv, and no pun intended there. You crossed the line and you can't go back, and you might as well enjoy it. If it's going to end awkwardly, then whether you just kiss or whether you have screaming sex ten times a day for the next week and a half isn't going to change that outcome. But you could have a blast in the meantime."

It sounds so logical, but it doesn't chip away at the panic building in my chest.

"Liv," she says sternly. "This isn't Zeke. This isn't some guy making you believe he's going to give you forever and then stomping all over your heart."

"I wish you wouldn't do that."

"What?"

"Give Zeke so much power. He was an asshole."

"He was an asshole you were in love with."

"But I'm not anymore."

Eve narrows her eyes at me. "That doesn't mean he isn't still in there, messing with your head."

"He's not."

"Have it your way," she says, shrugging. "Either way, this thing with Chase isn't anything like that. It's a once-in-a-life-time opportunity to do something crazy, knowing full well that it has an expiration date. You move to Golden; you get a nice, clean break from whatever weirdness might arise. Everything doesn't have to be serious. It's the twenty-first century! Women get to have casual sex, too."

I don't say anything.

"Liv. You can't tell me you don't want to take a ride on that coaster before you head out of Disneyland!"

I start giggling and can't stop. That starts her giggling, too, then outright laughing, until she has to grip the table to keep from tipping over and the people around us in the diner are giving us weird looks.

"God! I can't believe you're leaving! I am going to miss you so darn much!"

"Me, too. You have to come visit all the time."

She has tears in her eyes. Eve doesn't cry, so that makes me cry. The other people in the diner have given up on making sense of us and returned to their conversations.

"And you have to come back all the time."

We promise. We actually pinky-swear, which makes us both laugh and then cry some more.

16

CHASE

"How's the business plan coming?" Brooks asks me.

We're having lunch today with his brother, Sawyer—the one with the kid and the dead wife—and Brooks's friend Jack. Jack's a general contractor and the site where he's working is close by. Sawyer builds furniture from recycled wood and works on his own schedule—so theoretically he could join us for lunch any time—but Brooks has to do a bit of convincing to get him to crawl out of his grief cave.

I shrug in response to Brook's question. "Business plan, meh. I mean, I'm pounding away at the basics. But I don't feel like I have that one winning concept that's going to blow Mike's nephew away."

"These guys both run their own businesses. You should toss your thoughts at them, see if they have ideas for you."

"What's the situation?" Jack asks.

I catch Jack and Sawyer up on the fact that I'm competing against Mike's nephew to buy the store.

"Ah. That's a setup," Jack says, frowning. "Especially with his wife already having made up her mind."

"But Chase knows the business inside and out," Brooks says. "He's totally got this."

That's the thing about Brooks—he can be a pain in the ass, but he's also loyal as hell.

"So what are you thinking?" Jack asks.

"We have to get a lot more stuff online," I tell them. I've been thinking about this, and as with most businesses, we can't just be a local outfit anymore. We have to get more reach than that. "But just because I put more merchandise online doesn't mean it'll be easy to get people to choose us over one of the big, well-known retailers, especially when we don't have a rep. I think we need some partners. People who'll refer customers to us. Businesses that run trips, especially."

"What about the Wilders?" Brooks asks Sawyer.

Sawyer shrugs. He's a man of few words, and from what I understand from Brooks, far fewer words this last year or so. "Don't see why not."

Brooks explains to Chase and me, "We grew up in Bend, Oregon area with these guys, the Wilder brothers, and they run a pretty sizable outdoor adventure company. Gabe's a great guy. He and Sawyer are still tight."

"Good name," says Jack, whose son is also Gabe. "We can call him Big Gabe to keep things straight."

"When you meet this guy, you'll see he's not the kind of guy you give a nickname to."

"Okay," Jack says. "My Gabe can be Little Gabe, for now. But I'm planning on him growing up to be the kind of guy no one wants to give a nickname to, either."

As a fellow dad, I totally appreciate this sentiment.

"Would you mind putting me in touch with Gabe?" I ask Sawyer.

He shrugs again. "Sure. Give me a couple days."

"Yeah, no problem."

"How's my favorite nephew doing?" Brooks asks Sawyer.

"Jonah's okay," Sawyer says.

"You know you're in good company with these two, right?" Brooks cocks his head to indicate Jack and me. "It's the single dad survival club around here."

"Jack's not single," I point out. Jack recently got back together with the mother of his kid—and he's been whistling and staring giddily into space for months straight.

"No," Jack says, grinning. "Jack's not single."

"You've got the cocky glow of a guy who's getting laid regularly," Brooks tells Jack. "Whereas, you two look like shit." He aims this last at Sawyer and me.

Sawyer and I both glare at his brother.

Brooks's eyes narrow on me. "Sawyer has an excuse," he says. "What's yours? Liv refusing to let you go on dates?"

"I went on a date. Saturday night."

Brooks eyes me suspiciously. "Couldn't have been much of a date," he says. "You have the strained look around the eyes that comes from overly much acquaintance with your right hand."

I ball up my napkin and aim it at him, but he ducks and I miss.

"How are things with Liv?" Jack gives me a searching look. I realize that any and all attempts to dodge what's taking up all the space in my head is sure to be sussed out by one of these guys before the check comes. So I might as well get their thoughts. I'm sure as hell not going to figure this out by myself.

"Question for you," I say. "Do I instantly lose all credibility as a human being if I mess around with the nanny? Even if she's temporary?"

All mouths drop open. Even Sawyer is staring at me incredulously now.

Brooks looks like his eyes are going to pop out of his head. "You? And Liv? Haven't you told us a thousand times that that would never happen, not in a million years?"

"That's too much math for me," Jack mutters.

I hang my head. "I might've been wrong about that."

Jack shifts in his seat. "The under-one-roof thing is potent."

I know there's a whole story of what happened when circumstances pushed him and Maddie—his kid's mom—under the same roof... but I've never pressed him to tell it. I make a mental note to ask.

I tell my friends a brief version of what happened between me and Liv.

The three of them are openmouthed when I'm done.

I can't really blame them. The story sounds outrageous when spoken out loud.

Jack tilts his head, scrutinizing my face. "You were jealous," he accuses.

I open my mouth to deny it, then close it. He's fucking right. I was jealous. Jealous that Liv had been open to the idea of Kieran visiting her in Golden, jealous of the fact that she'd kissed him. Jealous, jealous, jealous.

"That's why she got pissed at you," Jack says. "No one wants the jealous possessive kiss."

"Oh, and *you* never did that shit," Brooks mutters to Jack.

"I learned from my mistakes." Jack crosses his arms.

"And now you have a podcast about how to be a kickass boyfriend."

Jack rolls his eyes. "He's full of shit. I don't have a fucking podcast." Then he turns back to me. "Look, I gotta ask this. Don't get mad."

I frown. "Nothing that starts that way ever ends well."

"Is it possible you're just looking for someone to help you raise your kid? I mean, if things work out between the two of you, you have a built-in mommy figure for your girl—"

"No."

That shuts him up. And makes Brooks' eyebrows go up.

"I mean, I love that she makes Katie happy. Not gonna lie. But she's leaving, so she can't fill that role. I'm not looking at this as a long-term thing. I'm just trying to figure out what I do for the next two weeks, when she's here. Do I try to stay away—?"

I get a vivid flashback to naked Liv.

"What?" Brooks demands.

"I may or may not have accidentally seen her naked," I admit.

"So maybe that's it," Jack says. "You can't get the eye candy out of your head."

"No," I insist. "I mean, yeah, she's hot as fuck, but it's not that. She's—"

Fun. Funny. Strong. Kind.

A good person.

"I like her," I say lamely.

All three men exchange glances.

"What!?" I demand.

"Are you sure this is a good idea?" Brooks asks, more gently than I think I've ever heard him. "I mean, with her leaving."

"That's what *makes* it a good idea. Because whatever happens, it can't get too complicated."

Brooks narrows his eyes at me again.

"Don't delude yourself," Jack says suddenly. "You can lie to everyone else, but you need to be honest with yourself."

"Podcast," Brooks tells him. "You'll make a fortune."

Jack gives him a leisurely, good-natured middle finger.

"Or maybe YouTube channel," Brooks muses. "You could invite guests. You could name it Dr. Jack. Dr. Jack's Love Formula."

"You're just jealous," Jack says.

Brooks smirks. "Of the fact that you'll never have sex with another woman again? Hardly."

I expect Jack to come back with a scathing retort, but he just grins, the self-satisfied grin of a man who doesn't have to depend on himself for satisfaction.

"So what does Dr. Jack's Love Formula have to say about Chase's dilemma?"

"Well," Jack says. "You said it yourself, Chase. You like her."

He leans on the word *like*, and I frown.

"She's my friend. Who I'd like to investigate benefits with."

"Just know what you're getting yourself into. If you have feelings for her—"

"I don't have feelings," I say. "Not like *feelings* feelings."

"I'm telling you, YouTube Channel interviews," Brooks murmurs. "You'll make a fortune."

We both give him the finger.

Jack squints at me. "I guess I'm just saying that if you think there's a chance these are *feelings* feelings and not just sexytimes feelings, and she's leaving in less than two weeks, maybe that's a good reason to keep it in your pants. For both of your sakes."

Sawyer has been quietly listening this whole time, but now he clears his throat.

We all turn to look at him, because—well, I think we all feel like if the guy who doesn't talk has something to say, we should probably listen. And even if unmarried guys give married guys shit, maybe we do think they might know something we don't.

Sawyer's been married *and* widowed—he's like the king of guy wisdom.

His voice is rough, like it's rusty from disuse. He sounds pissed.

"Life's really fucking short."

I'm not easily intimidated, but Sawyer's one of those guys —the strong silent type—that could murder you in your sleep if he turns out to be a bad guy. I flinch back a bit, waiting for his next pronouncement, but it doesn't come. He just shuts his mouth and lowers his eyes and goes back to a distant place.

That's it. That's all he had to say.

And in the wake of that, we're *all* silent, thinking about it, until the waitress breaks the awkward moment by bringing out food, and then we spend the rest of lunch talking about shit that doesn't matter, because *no one* wants to go there again with Sawyer.

I LEAVE THE STORE EARLY, figuring there's no way, after what happened last night, that Liv will want to help me cook for my parents. And that's fine. I'll stop home, check in on Katie, and head to the grocery store.

So I'm shocked when I pull into the driveway and discover Liv unloading grocery bags from Eve's car. Shocked, and ridiculously glad to see her. "I thought you'd bail."

Her eyes fly up to meet mine, startled. "I told you I'd help you with the dinner. And I will."

Her tone is brusque, though. Businesslike.

"You don't have to." My words come out curt, too.

"I'm not doing it because I have to." She begins unpacking the bags efficiently, briskly, putting stuff away in the refrigerator and the cabinets as easily and comfortably as if she were in her own kitchen. I can't help it; I like it. I like that she feels that comfortable in my kitchen, that it's almost like she—

Like she lives here.

I think of my friends, exchanging glances, telling me not to delude myself.

Feelings feelings.

They're not onto something, are they?

Are they?

She comes back to where I'm standing, hands on hips. "Let me try that again. I want to help you with this dinner. After all, I am your friend." She laughs, a short, unamused laugh. "Even if you are a total idiot."

I recognize an opening when I hear one. "I am a total idiot," I admit. "I did that all wrong."

"What are you saying?" She narrows her eyes.

"I shouldn't have—" No, that's not what I mean. Not what I mean at all. "I should never have made you feel like I was kissing you to prove a point. I wasn't. Not at all."

"You weren't?"

Does she sound . . . hopeful? And is the hope in her voice and on her face starting a cascade of that same emotion in my chest?

Life's really fucking short. Sawyer's rusty voice.

"Nope."

"Then why were you doing it?"

Her eyes are huge, fixed on my face. The moment feels super-charged.

"Because I wanted to."

Her expression is a question. I have to stop myself from grabbing her and kissing her. I have to tell her the whole truth first.

"I kissed you because I wanted to kiss you. Because I wanted you. Want you. And I'm sorry if I made you think it was for any other reason."

"Oh," Liv says. "Wow." Her cheeks are pink. She bites her lower lip, which makes me want to lean in and lick the bitten spot. And kiss the hell out of her.

"But I shouldn't have. You were seeing someone else. I messed up."

"Wait," she says.

I stop.

"I, um—I broke it off with Kieran."

I'm so startled, I can't stop my eyes from flicking to her face.

"Like, before you kissed me. I already had."

Her eyes are on mine. Soft and uncertain, a darker green

than usual. And hope leaps back to life in me, with an accompanying surge of need.

"Because he was a lousy kisser?"

She bites her lip again. And then nods. And smiles. A small, secret, sexy smile.

I feel an answering flare in every blood vessel in my body.

"Daddy, can I watch *Frozen*?"

All the air goes out of the moment. It's like we were both holding our breath and when Katie stepped in, we exhaled.

It's both a relief and a disappointment.

I glance at Liv. She looks dazed—the way I feel—like Katie broke a spell.

"Let's find something else for you to do," I tell Katie, and she races out of the room ahead of me, probably all eager to turn me into a princess again.

As I'm following her out, I turn back.

Life is really fucking short.

"I kissed you because I wanted to," I repeat to Liv, because saying it felt so good and because the color high in her face makes her look even more beautiful than usual. "And unless you tell me you don't want me to, I'm going to do it again."

17

LIV

The doorbell rings—Chase's parents must be here. I'm up to my elbows in cooking, and that's probably a good thing. I'd rather hang back and let Chase and Katie get the door. I've got a lot to think about. Like how much I want Chase to kiss me again—and how much I shouldn't.

In the foyer, Katie squeals, and unfamiliar voices fuss and coo over her, telling her how big she is, how old she's gotten, how pretty the pink dress she and I picked out looks on her.

"It's a party dress," I hear Katie tell them.

"Of course it is!" the woman's voice says.

Chase leads his parents into the kitchen, Katie skipping alongside, and I'm—surprised. In that way you're surprised when you don't even know what you were expecting, you just know this isn't it.

"Mom, Dad, this is Liv. Liv, my parents, Frannie and Sidney Crayton."

"So nice to meet you, Liv," Mrs. Crayton says, extending

her hand. She's tall and slim and absolutely gorgeous in an expensive way—styled ash-blond hair, diamond-stud earrings, makeup, white capris and a melon-colored flowy tank top, heels and polished toes, and toned, tanned arms. And Mr. Crayton is her perfect partner—meticulously trimmed silver hair, beard, and mustache, linen shirt, tailored slacks, and shoes that can't have cost less than $500. He shakes my hand, too, with a restrained nod of greeting.

I guess it's the expensive or maybe the tailored that surprises me. Chase is so outdoorsy, sporty, down-to-earth, and, in his own words, low maintenance, I guess I figured his parents would be more like him.

"Liv's a good friend of mine, and she's helping Katie and me out while we look for a new nanny. She'll be here a couple of weeks and then she's leaving for Golden. She got another nanny job. She's terrific with kids—she's been amazing with Katie."

There's pride in Chase's voice, and for some reason that warms me to the core.

"Nana and Papa, we're having sketti with meat sauce and Liv is making the sauce!"

"It's very kind of you to cook for us," Mrs. Crayton says. "Chase says it's not in your job description."

That makes me smile. "Oh, it's my pleasure."

We offer them drinks and stand awkwardly for a moment.

It's funny. I think if I'd met Chase's parents before tonight, I might have suggested a different dinner menu. They seem more like the tofu stir-fry set than the spaghetti-with-meat-sauce set. I set out the chips and salsa and guac, wishing I had made lemon hummus and served it with crudité. But what can you do? They're gracious and obviously grateful for what we have put in front of them.

They ask me a whole bunch of polite questions—what's the job I'm going to, where I'm from originally (I always say the Boston suburbs, because that's where most of my foster homes were), how I'm planning to get to Golden. I answer as best I can as I finish putting dinner together. In turn, I ask them how their trip is going, and they tell me all about the San Juan Islands and Vancouver and Victoria—all places I've never been.

Chase is surprised I've never been to the San Juan Islands. He starts quizzing me about other Pacific Northwest destinations—Portland; Cannon Beach, Oregon; the Washington coast; the Olympic Peninsula; the North Cascades. When he discovers I've never been to the North Cascades National Park, he says, "That is a crime against humanity."

"That's putting it pretty strongly," I say, amused.

"It's the best backcountry camping in the U.S."

I scrunch my nose, because Chase, of all people, knows how I feel about camping. I'm about to say so when his mother interjects, "Chase, dear, not everyone likes camping. Some of us value civilization."

Oh. I remember what he told me yesterday, about feeling "real" or "alive" when he was outside and trapped inside. When he talked about hunting and camping and fishing, he said that he did those things with his uncle.

There is more than one way to feel like you don't belong. Bouncing from foster home to foster home definitely made me feel that way. But clearly Chase felt that way in his own home, growing up.

Normally I might have jumped in to agree with his mom about the lures of civilization, but for some reason I say, "Sounds amazing."

"It is," Chase says, and there's little-boy-at-Christmas excitement in his voice.

The food is ready, so we make our way to the table and sit down. Katie wants her grandparents to sit on either side of her, which doesn't take much convincing. I'm expecting Katie to need me to cut her spaghetti, but she asks her grandfather to do it, and he obliges. I'm charmed, watching him, all groomed and dignified but totally doting on Katie.

"So, Chase," his mother says. "How are things going? You need help with anything? Are you getting the rent paid on time?"

Wha—? I shoot Chase a quick glance. Like, Something I don't know about? As far as I know, Chase doesn't have money troubles or any issues like that at all.

He rolls his eyes. Ignore her, the look says. "Mom. I'm on it."

"You getting yourself to work on time?" his dad asks, handing Katie her fork. "You stepping up when you have a chance to take stuff on?"

"Yeah, Dad, of course," Chase says. "Work's good."

"Chase is working on trying to buy the store," I say. Because Jesus, they're both making it sound like they expect Chase to be barely functional at his job and his life, when he and I both know he's a superstar. Good enough to be heir apparent at the store. And I want him to know I'm proud of him the way he's proud of me.

It doesn't have exactly the result I'm expecting, though. Instead of looking proud, both of Chase's parents look worried. "Don't bite off more than you can chew," Chase's mom says, and his dad says, "You don't have to prove anything to us, son. We know how far you've come."

And again, I'm like, wha—? They're asking these questions, saying this stuff, that doesn't make any sense to me. It's as if they think he's a kid who can't tie his shoes. He's twenty-fucking-eight, and the Chase I know can more than take care of himself and whomever else needs taking care of. He's running the store, raising his daughter, and hosting his parents for dinner. Why can't they see how competent he is?

"If I buy the store—and that's a big if—I'll make sure I know exactly what I'm getting myself into," Chase says, a lot more patiently than I think either of his parents deserves.

"We want you to know, Chase, we're so proud of you."

"I know, Mom."

He shoots me a sideways glance that's full of humor, and I realize: This is old hat to him, and isn't bothering him nearly as much as it's bothering me. This conversation happens all the time between him and them. I really don't understand.

"What about you guys?" Chase asks. "Heard anything about how the company's doing?"

His parents begin talking, and it doesn't take me long to piece it together. Apparently, they ran a local grocery delivery service until maybe five years ago, when they sold it. And his dad is not happy with the people who bought it. They're running it into the ground. They're incompetent, they're greedy, and it sounds like they might be unethical, too.

And the longer his dad talks, the more Chase's jaw tightens, and I can't help the feeling that if his dad doesn't shut up soon, Chase is going to say something he'll regret.

But it doesn't happen. Instead, Chase's mom changes the

subject and starts asking Katie about what she and I do together when Daddy is at work. Katie is thrilled to be asked an adult question and launches into a whole speech.

We all turn our focus to Katie, and the moment passes.

18

LIV

"What was that about?"

Chase just got back downstairs from putting Katie to bed. His parents left to go back to their hotel—they're flying out at the crack of dawn tomorrow—so it's just the two of us in the living room now.

"What was what about?"

"When your dad was talking about the guys who took over the business. And you looked like you wanted to take a bite out of someone."

He shrugs, but I know Chase, and I don't buy it.

"Seriously, Chase."

"It's nothing."

I wait. I'll wait all night if I have to, and I can see him starting to get uncomfortable in the silence. Finally, he says, "It's a long story, Liv. And water under the bridge."

"Didn't look like water under the bridge."

He shrugs. "It just pisses me off." He tugs at a loose thread at his sleeve. "When he talks that way about it. Because I could have kept all that from happening if he'd left me the business. Or even sold me the business."

"Why didn't he?"

Chase folds his arms and looks away. "He didn't think I could hack it."

"What do you mean he didn't think you could hack it?"

"Are you sure you want to open this can of worms?"

I nod.

"I had a tough time as a kid, which means they had a hell of a time with me. ADHD and a whole card deck of undiagnosed learning disabilities. Didn't learn to read till I was almost ten. It's still slow going for me if I have to read anything long."

He pauses, as if waiting for me to react. It's startling but not, somehow, shocking. I mean, Chase is a crazy-smart guy, but not a book-smart guy—the other kind. It doesn't make me think any less of him that he's not book smart, not when I know how capable he is in so many ways. I've seen firsthand what a great dad he is, and I know how much Mike values his work at the store.

His eyes search mine, and there's a look in them—as if he's still waiting for my disappointment—but he takes a breath and goes on.

"Homework was hell. Projects were hell. Teachers couldn't handle me; I got kicked out of elementary school and then out of the private school my parents tried next. My mom homeschooled me for a while, and then she couldn't handle me, so they sent me to a different private school, and —the short version is that my parents have always seen me as that kid. Troublemaker, class clown, not going anywhere. They sent my brother to Yale and didn't even talk to me about college. Which is—I mean, I get it. I didn't do anything to challenge their assumptions. But it still stung when they sold the business instead of giving me a shot at running it."

"I can see why," I say quietly. I sit down across from him on the couch.

"They wanted Henry—that's my older brother, you'll probably meet him at some point—to take over the business, but he went and got a medical degree and became an emergency room doc. He was basically their perfect son, except for the not-taking-over-the-business part. And I guess I assumed it would be mine, since it wasn't his. When my dad told me he was selling it instead of passing it along to me, he said, 'You have no idea how much it hurts me not to be able to pass this business on to one of my sons, but it would kill me to watch someone else destroy what I've worked my whole life to build.'"

I flinch. "Jesus, Chase, that is so unbelievably harsh. What kind of dad—?"

"A dad who meant it," he says quietly, and my heart squeezes.

"That's why you don't trust yourself to do the business plan."

He closes his eyes. "Yeah. I've been working on the plan. Chipping away at it. But, yeah. I have trouble imagining that I stand a chance against this other guy. Whose dad, I'm sure, would have given him the family business."

I reach out and take his hand. Squeeze it. Run a thumb gently over his skin, loving the way it's both smooth and unmistakeably masculine. "Why don't you get in their faces and tell them it's bullshit, the way they see you? The way they talk about you?"

He shakes his head. "Because I don't have to. It doesn't matter how they see me. I know who I am, and what I'm capable of. Once I knew Thea was pregnant, I did everything I could to get my act together. I doubled down on all the tutoring and therapy and medication and meditation that people had been trying to get me to take seriously for years. Even more to the point, I started taking responsibility for myself. And I did it. I figured out how to be a competent adult and a good dad. That's who I am now, and that's what I focus on. If I didn't, I wouldn't have let Katie come live with me. If I thought I wasn't capable or competent to support her and raise her, you better believe in a split second I'd have found another place for her. My parents wanted to take her. They tried to convince me they should. But I said no. I said this was the right place for her. And I believe that."

My mouth is all but hanging open in disbelief. "They— they said they should take her instead of you?"

He nods.

"Chase, how can they— That's—" I'm speechless. Sputtering.

"God knows I wish they saw me as I am and not as I was, but to be fair to them, there was a time in my life I had trouble keeping a goldfish alive. They felt like they'd be lucky if I ever moved out of their place, let alone held down a job and supported my kid. They give me a little more credit each time they see me, but it's going to take years before I fully convince them I've got this. But it's okay, Liv. It's really okay. I know I've got this."

The thing is, I can tell he means it.

"Chase. You're—amazing. You tossed all that off like it's not a big deal, but you turned your life around, went from being a guy whose own parents didn't trust him to inherit the family business to being a guy whose boss wants him to take over his. So when you're working on this business plan, you have to remember that. That you're *not* the guy your dad said all that shit to anymore. Not at all. I mean, the whole time they were talking about you at dinner, it was like they were talking about someone else completely. I couldn't recognize that guy."

The look on his face—I haven't seen anything like it before. I thought I liked it when his face was all hunger and need, but this is something else. This softness. This... gratitude.

"Chase," I whisper.

"Chase. You know how you asked me why I get with guys I'm not really into?"

He squints. "Yeah. Sorry about that."

"No. You were right. It's true. I do date guys I'm not that into."

"I do date guys I'm not that into," Liv says.

There's something in her voice. And a little curve to the corner of her mouth. She's serious, but she's teasing, too. My heart pounds.

She bites her bottom lip. "I'm getting kind of sick of it, though. You want to help me break the habit?"

She's crawling toward me on the couch, and holy fuck. My body starts to react long before she reaches me, blood surging in my veins. By the time she straddles me, one knee on either side, I'm so hard it's as much pain as pleasure. She's wearing a blue dress I've never seen before, and it rides up around her waist so all that's between us is her panties and my jeans. I can feel her heat.

"Yeah," I tell her. Because, yeah.

"Mmm," she says, rubbing herself against me.

I cup her head and draw her mouth down to mine. Her lips are so soft, and she smells unbelievably good. I coax her open and explore her mouth with my tongue, savoring her slickness, her taste. I'm going down on this girl. Maybe not right this second, but only because I can't stop kissing her, delving into her mouth, loving the slide of her tongue against mine and the clutch of her hands on my shoulders.

She breaks it off, and for a split second I'm afraid she's going to freak out and call a halt again, but she just says, "About Kieran's kissing."

"Yeah?"

She sighs. "The whole time, I'm thinking, *Too dry. Too wet. Too sloppy. Too restrained. Too scratchy. Too peckish.* I can't shut down my brain."

I want to smile. Part of it is the word peckish, but mainly it's the pleasure of hearing her admit what I'd guessed. But I don't smile. Instead I say, cool as a cucumber, casual as can be, not displaying one iota of how important the question feels, "And when I kiss you?"

She closes her eyes, and her lips part.

Jesus Christ, I thought I was as hard as it was possible to be, but I guess not. "When you kiss me . . ."

I think I hold my breath.

"Everything in my whole body wants to give itself to you." She opens her eyes and lets me see the heat there.

"Oh, fuck," I say, involuntarily.

That makes her smile. Just a slight turning up of the corners of her mouth, but it sweeps away the rest of my restraint.

I wrap her in my arms and drop my mouth onto hers. Hers opens and softens under mine. She tastes like—

Her. A taste so familiar you'd think this was way more than our second kiss.

We kiss and kiss, my tongue finding hers and refusing to stop relishing its sweetness. Her body comes into line with mine, her nipples hardening against my chest like I imagined, my aching cock snugged between us. It's not only my cock that aches. I ache all over, and I try to bring her closer and hold more of her as if that will help—but it only amps up my hunger, particularly because she is pressing back and wiggling against me like she's trying to get closer too. Her fingers are plunged into my hair and she's whimpering into my mouth. The effect on my body of her humming against my sensitive flesh is electric.

She pulls at my T-shirt, sliding her hands under it. They're warm and relentless, exploring me everywhere, her fingertips circling my nipples and sifting through my hair. She tries to get the T-shirt off. "Chase," she groans.

Obviously we need to get ourselves behind a closed door as soon as humanly possible. I stand up with her still in my arms, her legs wrapped around my waist, where I feel like they belong. "Upstairs."

I carry her up the stairs and down the hall, depositing her on my bed, which I—miraculously, luckily—made this morning. It looks terrific with her on it. Her lips are red, her cheeks flushed, her knees parted, her dress pushed up high enough that I can see the edge of her panties. I lean down, set my mouth there, and kiss along the hem of the dress.

I catch the scent of her arousal, rich and salty, and my dick throbs.

"Chase," she murmurs as I push her hem higher, revealing a pair of barely there black lace panties.

"You know what you remind me of right now?"

She shakes her head, eyes wide.

"A present. A really sexy present. And you know what I want to do to you?"

Her eyes gleam. She's into this, into me, which is such a turn-on. "What?"

"Unwrap you and fuck you."

For a moment I think I've gone too far, but then she releases a breath that's more moan than air, a moan I feel to the bottom of my soul.

"Yes, please," she whispers.

20

LIV

His eyes are dark. Hard. Hot. Relentless—he won't let me look away. He traces a finger up and down my sex through the lace, which is soaked through.

I can't help it, I moan. And arch, lifting myself to get more of his touch. To get it where I need it.

He pulls his hand back. Bastard. I want that hand under my panties. I want my panties gone, far, far away. I want—

"You're so wet. Were you thinking about this? During dinner? In the living room?" he demands.

All I can do is nod.

"Good." He gives me a look of pure male triumph, then grabs my ankles and pulls me to the edge of the bed.

"These are in the way," he says, tugging my panties down. He pulls my legs up over his shoulders, settling between them. He kneels at the side of the bed and kisses my thigh, nibbling, breathing warmth that tingles everywhere. My nipples are so tight they hurt. Then he gives the other thigh the same treatment. He works his way up, alternating. "God, you smell good. Do you taste as good as you smell?"

His mouth is on me, soft, hot, skilled—his tongue circling to my center, then widening out. He is patient and relentless and unbelievably good at his craft, and he builds me up so slowly and steadily, the sensation beginning to spiral out, bigger and bigger, pulling more and more of me in, until I am coming, bucking as he holds my hips down, as he flattens one hand over my stomach and licks the last of my orgasm out of me.

"You taste even better than you smell," he says, a self-satisfied smile on his face as he regards the slick mess of his handiwork.

All I can do is hum my approval. I'm throbbing so deeply and so thoroughly that it's hard to think about anything else.

"Can I fuck you?"

I choke out a moan.

"Is that a yes?"

He lunges for the nightstand drawer, liberates a square of foil, and drops it on the bed.

He pulls his T-shirt over his head.

"Wait. I want to look at you."

His eyes meet mine, startled, and his face flushes. He stands by the side of the bed, not flexing or showing off, just letting me look. I slowly peel my limp rag of a self off the bed and run my hands over all the contours of his torso—the ridges in his abs, the taunting trail of hair, the hard-spun muscles that form his chest and shoulders and arms. And he lets me, his eyes closing in a fierce pleasure that makes me feel strangely, disturbingly tender.

I kneel up on the bed and touch my mouth to one of his nipples, then the other, and now it's his turn to groan. "Liv—"

I trace the kiss down the center of his chest, down the center valley of his abs, to his navel, my tongue dipping in.

"Oh, Jesus, Liv, no, don't." He cups my face in his hands. "I will come before you can get your mouth on me." He releases me and reaches into his jeans, adjusting himself, creating a gorgeous ridge under the denim and a tantalizing gap where his waistband no longer meets his skin.

His threat only eggs me on, because the idea of making Chase lose control dissolves my sanity.

I dip my tongue into the gap where his erection has distended his waistband and find him there, velvet and salty.

"Oh, shit," he says, but doesn't pull away.

I reach for the top button of his jeans, undo it. Then the zipper, until I can free him from his jeans and his briefs. I admit to myself that I have been anticipating this moment from the first clash of my hip against his erection yesterday. And he doesn't disappoint. Long and thick and dark and swollen, the cut head plump and slick from pre-cum and my tongue. I can't resist ducking my head again and swirling my tongue around him.

"Can I tell you something?"

His voice is thick and rough.

I nod, and swirl again.

"I've been fantasizing about this."

"This in particular? Me giving you head?"

His eyes darken. "You giving me head. When I saw that photo of you with the ice cream cone. When you were crouched on your froggie lily pad the other day, gazing up at me in worship."

I stick my tongue out at him, and he waggles his eyebrows.

"That's a lot of thinking about me blowing you. I hope it lives up."

I lie down on my belly on the bed—still in my dress, which will have to be dry-cleaned—and open my mouth, open to him, and take him as deep as I can.

"Oh, fucking fuck, Liv, yes, Jesus, yes."

The longing in his wrecked voice makes me ache so much that I almost ask him to fuck me, but then his cock swells against my tongue and I double down on plan A. I'm still throbbing deep from what his mouth did to me moments ago, and I can feel myself getting wetter and more swollen as I work him up and down, my hand stroking his balls and the base of his cock. He tenses, his thighs, his abs, his glutes clenching under my palms as I guide him to slide in and out between my slick lips.

"Liv." His voice is urgent, and he tries to pull away, but I hold him close. "Liv, I want to be inside you."

I pull back, and he swipes a thumb over the shine on my lips, then reaches for the condom he dropped on the bed. I watch eagerly as he rolls it down over his shiny, swollen cock —his eyes never leaving my face.

"Lie back," he says.

He enters me slow and sweet. Filling me, spreading me, opening me, inch by inch by inch by—

Yeah.

He watches me the whole time he's easing in, like he's reading his progress on my face, and when he's all the way inside me, he presses tight against my pubic bone and thrusts again, then circles his hips against mine. I gasp. It feels so unbelievably good.

I love the self-satisfied expression on his face.

"Hell yes," I whisper, and his eyes go a fraction darker.

"You feel really good." His voice is rough. His hips circle again, drawing another gasp out of me. He's braced over me, muscles tensed with effort. When he pulls back and thrusts again, his abs brush against my belly, and my internal muscles clench, as if in greeting. His lids droop at the sensation, so I squeeze him again deliberately, and he narrows his gaze at me. "Don't," he says.

So I do.

"Liv," he warns.

"What?" I ask innocently, doing it again. He shouldn't be having all the fun.

"You're going to make me come."

"Yeah, I am."

"Not yet," he grunts. "Don't. Want. It. To. Be. Over. Yet."

I feel his words all over my body, tingling across my skin, heating my throat and chest, slicking the place his body fills me. I don't want it to be over yet, either, but I love this Chase, cocky but breakable.

We've caught a rhythm now, his hips riding mine, grinding those taunting circles against me, my clit swollen and sensitive and buzzing with pleasure. Every time he circles me, I squeeze around him, wanting desperately to make him lose his rhythm, his control.

He knows it, too, and our eyes are locked, every breath coming faster and faster. His rhythm falters, color rising high in his cheeks, his eyes closing briefly before he opens them and glares at me.

He flips us over so I'm on top, and I'm like, wait! Because Chase always wants to be in charge, so why is he giving up control to me?

Then he starts moving again, and I realize: Chase doesn't have to be on top to be in control.

He's thrusting up into me now, but the motion's the same —slow, controlled, the perfect friction, the perfect twist and grind. It's building pleasure up in me, steady and fierce.

And his hands are free.

He cups one breast in each hand.

"This," he says reverently, staring at my breasts over-flowing his palms, "is my happy place."

I can't help it—I giggle.

A moment later I'm not giggling at all. He finds my nipples with his thumbs and all of my concentration narrows in on the bright sensation of his callused skin moving lightly across the tight tips. A moan breaks out of me, then another, as the fire he's started in my breasts streaks downward through my belly, collecting, fierce, between my legs.

I want, want, want, want, and even though I'm a big girl and I know exactly what I'm chasing, I don't know what I want, either, it's that big and everywhere, and I clutch at him. I think I call his name, too.

"Livvy," he groans.

I come again, a glittery sensation like one of those fire-works that drip sparkles all over the sky. I swat his hands away from my nipples and thrust myself down on him as hard as I can, spasming around him. "So. Good," I tell him.

"Fuck," he says, rough and harsh, and then his eyes squeeze shut and his head tilts back and his mouth opens, roar-wide but silent, and his hand falls away from me to pound the mattress, his body rigid under mine. "Fuck, Livvy, fuuuuuuuuuuck."

I rest my head on his chest, listening to the pounding of his heart. His arms come around me.

When he gets up to throw out the condom, I get up, too, to go back to my room.

"Don't," he says.

So I don't.

21

CHASE

"**D**addy, wake up."

I regain consciousness unwillingly. I am alone in my bed. Katie's face is inches from mine.

My eyelids are gritty. My mouth is dry. My body feels like it's been worked over by a sadistic massage therapist. And still, the very first thing I do when I remember is grin.

Wow.

Wow, wow, wow.

Also, I think I tweaked a muscle in my butt. But the expression on Liv's face during the portion of the program that caused the butt injury definitely made it completely worthwhile.

"Daddy," Katie whines, startling me. Apparently I have closed my eyes and almost drifted back to sleep.

"It's too early, Katie," I say, full of hope. Sometimes this tactic works.

"It's seven thirty," she says sternly. "You are going to be late if you don't get up soon."

I confirm this with the bedside clock, and groan. I don't actually have to leave the house till 9:15, even when I'm opening. In a pinch, I can go from horizontal to sitting behind the wheel of the car in twenty minutes. Low maintenance, remember?

Just wait till Katie's a teenager and likes to sleep in. Then I will have my revenge.

I groan again and drag myself to sitting. "Is Liv awake?"

"I'll go wake her up."

"No, let her sleep."

I'm a morning person and Liv is not (Understatement alert!). And while before this morning I might have preferred to give her a hard time about that fact, even going so far as to deliberately unleash Katie on her, this morning, I am grateful and fond and, basically, rendered harmless by sex hormones.

I head down to the kitchen and fix Katie breakfast, setting her up so she can pour herself a second and third bowl of cereal and milk if she wants to. Then I head back upstairs to shower.

I whistle in the shower, as I shave, and even as I remake the bed, which is no mean feat because the sheets and covers are everywhere. Which makes me smile.

And makes me hard.

We're going to do that again. Tonight, if I have anything to say about it.

After the second round, we were both so blissfully wrecked that it would have been easy for us to crash out together in my bed. But we were both clear that we didn't want Katie to find Liv there in the morning. Too complicated. So I walked Liv down the hall and tucked her into her own bed. Then I came back in here, collapsed on the bed, and slept until Katie woke me.

Now I head down the hall and knock gently on Liv's door.

"Go away," says a craggy voice, unrecognizable as Liv's.

"I'm going to assume that greeting is about the amount of sleep you got and not about your feelings for me," I call through the door.

"My feelings for you are that you should go away," she says, muffled. "You can't come in. I look like ass. My hair's a mess. My makeup's a mess. I have pillow creases in my face."

"Let me see," I say.

"No."

"Please."

After a long, long silence—I've become totally convinced she's not going to let me in—she says, "Promise not to laugh."

I open the door.

She's sitting up, and she's right, technically: Her hair's a mess, her makeup is smudged, and she has pillow creases in her face. And it's possibly the sexiest thing I've ever seen, because I know that no one gets to see Liv like this.

"You look beautiful," I say, cupping her face. "I like you rumpled." I kiss her.

My strategy, if you can call it that, is not to give her any time to doubt me or overthink this. And it seems to be working, because she's kissing me back.

We tumble back into her covers. Her body is warm and limber against mine, and I'm hard against her thigh, her hands beginning to tug at my clothes, when I remember Katie. I break it off and stand up.

"You are evil," she says, panting. "You shouldn't start what you can't finish."

"Oh, I'll finish," I say. "Later. I promise. In the meantime, come downstairs. There's coffee."

"Coffee," she murmurs. "That might be better than an orgasm right now."

I check my watch, cross to the door, and jab the button in the center of the doorknob to lock it. I've got another minute or two before Katie finishes her breakfast, and a man can accomplish a lot in 120 seconds.

"Can't have you thinking that," I tell her.

22

LIV

I'm kind of weirded out by how not weird things feel.

I mean, we crossed a big line, right? This should be awkward. Or, just wrong. But instead we're sitting across from each other at the breakfast table, with Katie babbling between us, and it's normal. Me. Chase. Katie. A meal.

My body's still buzzing like crazy, because Chase made me come in about thirty seconds. I can't even make myself come in thirty seconds. But he did this thing with his tongue that I can't even explain, and—

Just thinking about it makes me hot all over.

"I'd better go grab a shower," Chase says, standing and clearing his plate. As he does, his cell rings on the counter, "Ode to Joy."

"Oh, hi, Em." He paces while he listens. "Um, I can't. Not today. I'll be at work. Unless—?" His eyes meet mine. "Hang on a sec." His arm, phone in hand, drops to his side. "I have a favor to ask."

"Shoot."

"Emily, Katie's other grandma, has an old friend visiting her from the East Coast, and she was wondering if I could drive Katie down, or at least halfway, so they could have lunch with her. Halfway would be an hour's drive; all the way would be close to two each direction. You could do some shopping or something while you wait for Katie to be done. I know it's a lot to ask—"

"It's fine," I say, meaning it.

Gratitude shines in his eyes. I like being able to make Chase's life easier, which is a funny thing, because so much of our friendship has been about giving each other a hard time.

Chase brings the phone back to his ear. "My friend Liv, who's filling in as Katie's nanny right now, can bring her." They talk back and forth for a minute or two about locations and logistics. Then he hangs up and lets me know where I'm heading with Katie, and when.

"You're going to have lunch with Grandma," he tells Katie, and she claps her hands in delight.

After Chase has showered and gone, I shower, then get Katie all ready for lunch. It's nothing fancy, some pizza place between here and Olympia that Chase and Emily agreed would be a good meeting spot, but I get her dressed up anyway so her grandmother can show her off. We play a few games of Hisss and Slamwich and get in the car.

Katie is dozy in the car on the way down, so I sing along to the radio. And—because I can't help myself—I relive moments of last night. It was so good. I want more.

Emily and her friend are waiting for us when we come in the front door of the pizza place, two older women in grandma jeans and T-shirts. Katie runs to the taller of the two and throws her arms around the woman's legs. Emily bends down and hugs Katie from above. She has curly gray hair and is older than I was expecting, seventy at least, brittle and skinny as a spider monkey.

She introduces Katie to her friend Grace and then thanks me, formally, for driving Katie down to lunch with them. She still hasn't introduced me to Grace. I'm familiar with the particular snub from nannying other times—people see you as not quite family, not quite a friend, just someone who moves the kid around for pay. And of course, that's exactly who I am in this situation.

The thing is, it would be totally different if I explained that I was Chase's friend first, and Katie's nanny only temporarily, as a favor.

And totally different, still, if I were Chase's girlfriend.

But I'm not.

I squat to check in with Katie. "You okay with staying here with your grandma and her friend while I do a little shopping? And I'll come back for you in an hour and a half?"

"Yeah!" says Katie.

I leave them alone and head to the mall for some window shopping—I don't want to spend any money—and a quick lunch. When I've finished demolishing my kale salad with apples and walnuts, I go to pick Katie up. Emily and her friend meet me in front of the pizza place with Katie, who is beaming. And bouncing.

"I had woot beer!" she tells me.

"Woot!" I say.

"And chocolate cake!"

"Woot, woot!"

Katie wrinkles her nose in confusion.

"I'm sorry to sugar her up and hand her back," Emily says, making eye contact with me for the first time.

"It's okay," I say, shrugging. "I get to strap her into the car. By the time we get home, the sugar rush will have worn off."

Emily smiles at that. Her face is creased and brown like a walnut, the skin of someone who's spent a lot of time in the sun. Her lips are thin, but not harsh. From the strength of the bones in her face, and from how pretty Katie already is, I can guess that Thea was gorgeous.

"Katie says you're her daddy's friend."

There's a heavy emphasis on the word friend. My face colors. Emily shoots her visitor a glance, as if my blush confirms something they both suspected. "How long have you and Chase been together?"

"We're not—" I stop. "It's not like that. We really are friends, just friends."

It's the truth. And a lie.

"I should have guessed," Emily says thoughtfully. "Chase doesn't have relationships, does he?"

I shake my head. And for some reason, what pops into my head is Chase sitting on the side of my bed this morning, telling me I was beautiful with my hair a rat's nest and my makeup a raccoon's mask.

I felt beautiful.

"I keep hoping he will. I know it's a strange thing for me to say, but I've always felt like Thea wasn't very fair to him, and maybe that's why he's so wary."

Emily's friend says, "Emily, hon—"

"Grace, I love—loved her, but it doesn't mean I approved of everything she did."

What I want to do, desperately, is ask her what she means.

About Thea not being fair to Chase. But what I say instead, because it's the only thing you can say to a mother who recently lost her daughter and still hasn't settled into the past tense, is, "I'm so sorry for your loss."

"Thank you, dear."

Grace puts a hand gently on Emily's arm. "We should get going."

"Yes." She turns to me, her eyes warm. "Thank you so much for bringing Katie. And I hope I'll see you next time I get together with Katie and Chase?"

I'll be in Golden, I think, but all I say is, "I hope so, too."

23

CHASE

That night, we each read Katie a book. Liv first, then me. And we say good night to Katie together.

When we're both settled in the living room afterward, Liv says, "I wasn't expecting Emily to be so old."

"She's sixty-eight."

"I guess because Thea had Katie so young—"

I shake my head. "Thea was twenty-eight when Katie was born."

Her startled eyes meet mine. "She was older than you."

"Yeah."

"I don't know why I thought—" Her look surfs off somewhere in the middle distance, then she seems to come back. "Emily said something . . ." She bites her lip. "She said Thea wasn't fair to you. And it surprised me. I don't know why, but I thought it was simpler than that. I thought it was a one-night thing, you got her pregnant, you guys decided to go your separate ways . . ."

I laugh. Harshly.

"No, huh?"

I shake my head.

"You want to tell me about it?"

"No."

"Will you tell me about it?"

I've never told anyone this story, not from the beginning. Obviously various people know bits and pieces of it—who Katie's mom was, the fact that we were never married. Brooks maybe knows the most, but even he doesn't know how it all started.

Somehow, though, I find myself telling Liv.

"Thea worked for my parents in Austin. She was their head of marketing. She was four years older than me. Polished, competent, confident.

"And I was—I already told you how I was. I'd just had that conversation with my father where he told me he wasn't leaving me the business, and I was in the process of self-destructing, like I was trying to prove him right."

She makes a sound like she's trying to contradict me, but I shake my head, and she nods, letting me continue.

"Thea came to dinner, and, like I said, she was so put together—I don't know if I was trying to stick it to my parents or if I wanted to see what she'd be like when she wasn't so in control, but I decided I was going to get her in bed."

I cast a look in Liv's direction, expecting to see judgment on her face, but she's listening patiently. And I realize that that's one of the things I like most about Liv, that she doesn't judge. She just takes it all in.

"Thea had just come off a serious relationship—I think he'd been about to propose, even—and she was going through some stuff of her own. And for some reason she dug the whole bad-boy thing. Or maybe it was the lure of sleeping with the bosses' kid; I don't know. She was on the rebound and she wanted to do something crazy, and I was offering the chance. So there we were, and that was all it was supposed to be, except for me, it wasn't."

Liv's mouth is open, a little. She closes it, then opens it again to say, "You fell in love with her."

"I fell in love with her." I shake my head. "Dumbest thing I've ever done."

"Hey, now. None of us falls in love with the wrong person on purpose." She gets a faraway look on her face, and there's sadness, too. Regret.

There's a story there, I think. I'm about to ask her about it, when she says, "And then she got pregnant."

"Well, no, that's not exactly how it happened. Not from my perspective."

She raises her eyebrows.

"She quit her job and moved to Seattle. Made it clear that she'd thought the whole time we were both having fun, blowing off steam. She didn't exactly say she'd been slumming it, but I knew that was what she meant. She broke my heart. Or, I thought she had. You know the punch line, though, so you know that wasn't the worst of it."

"So you let her walk away?"

She still hasn't gotten it. "She'd broken up with me. Told me she didn't have feelings for me. That was all. I couldn't change her mind."

The light dawns, her eyes widening. "Oh. God." She puts a hand to her chest. "She didn't tell you she was pregnant?"

"She didn't tell me," I confirm.

"How did you find out?"

"About eight months after that, my mother was at a

conference in Seattle and saw Thea with Katie in a front carrier. My mom wasn't close enough to talk to Thea, but she was close enough to be sure of what she'd seen. My parents never found out I'd been with Thea, so it didn't occur to my mom, when she told me she'd seen Thea with a baby, what a shock it would be. I lost my shit, freaked both of us out."

"God. Chase. That must have sucked."

I don't let myself think about the way it felt, getting hit with the truth. I make myself remember like I'm looking at the past through the wrong end of a telescope, remote and unconnected to me. "It did."

"Did you confront Thea?"

"I figured out where she was working and flew to Seattle to talk to her. I was as calm as I could be, and I asked to meet Katie, and then I asked Thea if she'd ever planned to tell me and she said no. And I asked why, and she wouldn't answer.

"But she didn't have to. I knew. She'd grown up with a dad who was a drunk and a deadbeat, and she'd told me, more than once, that it would have been better to have no dad at all."

A look of horror freezes on Liv's face. "She couldn't have been thinking that about you and Katie—"

It's a relief to see the anger and the hurt I felt back then reflected on Liv's face now. Like, there was no one to feel it for me or with me when it happened, but now there is, and that takes some of the pain away.

Liv shakes her head. "Even if she thought she didn't want you in their lives, she must have seen she was wrong. As soon as she saw you with Katie."

I shrug. "Yes and no. She came around, for sure. I moved here to be close to Katie, and that softened Thea a bunch.

And I got the job and cleaned up my life and did everything I could to be a good dad, and it made a difference."

"But?"

"But it was still tough to get time with Katie. I was supposed to have her Sundays and Mondays, and half the holidays, but I swear at least sixty percent of the time there was something in Katie's schedule that Thea couldn't work around. Thea wanted things exactly her way all the time. She thought Katie needed structure and consistency, and she didn't think I had anything to add to the life that she was making for her."

"Did you ever think about getting a lawyer?"

"Everyone I talked to said that it would take years and a fortune in bills, and that at best I'd carve out a little more time. And in the end, I felt like I couldn't do that to any of us, but most of all Katie. That money that I would have been spending, that money was Katie's. And as she got older, she would have known. That we were fighting over her."

"You're a good dad," Liv says quietly. "A really good dad. Whatever Thea believed about you, she was dead wrong."

It's one thing to know something for yourself. And it's another thing to have someone you care about say it to you. It settles in my chest, warm and exuberant and expanding. And I don't know what to do with it except to reach my arms out to her and say, "C'mere."

24

LIV

He draws me into his arms and kisses me. And I'm melting. Losing definition, losing edges. I whimper, which makes him clutch my head and kiss me harder, his tongue probing, then plundering.

"Upstairs," he says, but I'm having trouble letting him go —I have his hair and I keep pulling his face back to mine, and he keeps obligingly kissing me, until finally he tears himself away. "Upstairs," he repeats, in a tone of such complete command that it finally breaks through my sex haze and gets me off the couch.

"Your room," he says.

"Your bed is bigger."

"But I like your room more."

This is so un-Chase-like that I can't mount any kind of argument or even questioning. I follow him to my room, where he backs me up against the bed and then tips me onto it and follows me down, his thigh wedged between mine, his arms holding his weight off me except where I most want it. Mmm. We are dry-humping like horny teenagers and—

"Chase," I moan.

That makes him grin. He lowers his mouth to mine and keeps up the friction below, until it bursts like gold in me and I cry out into the kiss.

"You're so easy, and it is the sexiest thing ever," he says.

"I'm only easy because it's you," I say. Which is completely true. I'm never like this, uninhibited and push-button ready. Chase has the trip wire.

He kneels up over me and tugs his T-shirt off. I have to stare, because apparently I will never get enough of the visual spectacle that is Chase. The jeans come off next, and then his boxer briefs, and then he begins peeling me out of my clothes, and I'm too limp and glow-y to even help very much.

He pulls a condom out of his jeans pocket—

"Really?" I ask. "Were you a Boy Scout?"

"The Boy Scouts didn't want me," he says. "I was too out of control in meetings. But I'm way better at being prepared in all situations than a Boy Scout. The Boy Scouts ask me for help when they're out in the woods."

I don't doubt this. I take the condom out of his hand and tear it open. "You have a very—is it weird to say 'pretty'—cock?"

"Handsome?" he offers.

"Thick and curved just right, and—"

"Jesus," he says, snatching the condom back. "Keep that up and you'll never get as far as the condom."

"Nice fat head."

His eyelids are so heavy it's miraculous he can still see. "You didn't say you were a dirty-talker, too."

"Had to keep some surprises back."

He rolls the condom on, partially obscuring my view, but

it's okay because what comes next is better than the view. He lines himself, but then instead of plunging in, he plays. Tip of his cock against my super-sensitive clit, but he seems to know how lightly he has to stroke to keep me on the pleasure side of the pleasure-pain line. I drop my head back on the pillow and struggle to breathe.

"Tell me what you like."

"I like that," I say.

"And this?"

A finger, curled inside me, steadily stroking my g-spot. I moan my answer.

"And this?"

His mouth on mine and then slipping around to brush breath and teeth over the sensitive curls of my ear, along the slope of my jawline, across the bare skin of my throat, down to trap one nipple so it's held lightly between his teeth. His tongue comes out and flicks.

He plays. Finger, cock, tongue. The tension winds so tight in my low belly that I writhe and squirm and call his name, but he won't let me go over. Won't and won't and won't. I press my hips up, trying to get more, but he won't give it.

I'm past verbal. Can't even manage his name. Pushing my breast into his mouth, tipping my hips desperately, bearing down on the finger that is too thin to grab with my needy inner muscles. So riled I want to twist right out of his arms.

"You want to come?" He takes his mouth off my nipple long enough to ask, then ducks his head again.

I'm whimpering. It sounds almost like I'm crying, I'm that far gone out of my mind.

"Beg," he says, another pause in the nipple action.

"Please. Pleeaase."

"Tell me what you'll do if I make you come."

"I'll make you come. I'll suck you. I'll fuck you. I'll—I'll do anything. Anything you want me to do."

A look crosses Chase's face—and I get that rich, obscene thrill that I get from giving him pleasure. I'd do anything for that look. I open my mouth to promise more dirty things.

"Come camping with me."

"What?" It was so not what I expected him to say.

"Come camping with me."

"I don't camp."

He removes his mouth from my nipple. His cock from my clit. His finger from my pussy. He says, "Sure you do."

My muscles contract on emptiness and my nipples are cold from where he licked them. There's a fine burn in the deepest part of my belly that's already begging. "Fine. Whatever. I'll camp. Just make me come."

He gives me an absurdly triumphant look, then lines himself up again, and presses in. Slowly, so slowly. Farther and farther until he is buried to the hilt, and then he jacks his hips another half-centimeter, stroking his pubic bone over mine, and I come in such a rush that I almost pass out.

"Fuck!" he says, and his cock, already filling me so perfectly that I want to remember this moment forever, throbs and pulses while he throws his head back and closes his eyes and follows me over.

25

CHASE

"Y̲ou were kidding, right?" Liv whispers, after I've gotten up and thrown away the condom and come back to bed. She's lying in my arms, warm and relaxed, and I'm absurdly happy.

"About?"

"The camping." She scootches away from me so she can scrutinize my face.

"Dead serious."

"You can't seriously hold me to something I said when I was that out of my mind." She sounds genuinely alarmed, which makes me laugh.

"You promised. If I made you come, you'd do whatever I asked you to."

"I know, but we both know I meant, like, sexual stuff, favors, and I'm totally good for all that, any of that—"

I file that away for later, grinning.

"—but not camping."

"Holding you to it."

She buries her face in her hands. I feel a tiny bit sorry for her, and a lot triumphant. She raises her head. "Chase. You know me. You know I can't start the day without three cups of coffee and a hot shower. You know I don't go out in public unless I've had an hour and a half to do my hair and my makeup. You know I don't get dirty—"

I have many, many things to say about that, but I stick to the topic at hand. "Unless there's a kid involved," I point out. "I've seen you get all kinds of dirty doing craft projects and making mud pies."

"This is different. This involves not sleeping in a bed."

"I am all for not-sleeping in beds," I say, letting my hand drift down to cup her breast.

"You know that's not what I meant."

"Just for two nights. If you hate it you'll never have to do it again."

"I already hate it," she says.

"I need your help," I admit. "I want to take Katie camping. That's what dads do. They teach their kids to do the stuff they love. I love camping. And I want Katie to love camping. And I think it'll be a lot easier to do it the first time if you help me."

"I call bullshit," she says. "You're the manliest man in manland. You run a store called 'Mountainwear.' You can do anything you want to do."

What I said isn't the whole truth. I also want Liv to come with us because, well, because I want her there. I want to share what I love with her, too.

I am not, however, above exploiting the Katie element for my own gain. "I can't explain to a five-year-old girl how to pee in the woods without getting her shoes wet."

Liv closes her eyes and drops her head back, and I'm

pretty sure I've won, at least that round. I go in for the kill—
or that's my plan, anyway.

"I'll pay you. Double overtime."

She rolls her eyes. "Don't be ridiculous."

"You'll be working the whole time. And it'll be weekend
time."

She shakes her head. "Seriously, Chase, don't be stupid.
I'm not taking your money."

"But you'll do it?

She sighs heavily. Closes her eyes. Opens them again.

"Yeah. I'll do it." Her expression is bleak.

I feel a little bit sorry for her. But not really. Mostly I feel
elated. It's been way too long since I've camped, and I've
always wanted to take Katie. It wasn't the kind of thing I ever
could have convinced Thea to let me do, to give me Katie for
that long and to trust me not to screw it up.

I push away my old frustrations—Thea's gone now, and
there's no point in thinking about the past. I'm going to take
my girls camping, and we are going to have a great time.

Well, Katie and I are going to have a great time. I'm not
100 percent sure what Liv's going to think. But either way,
we'll have fun. Either Liv will fall in love with camping, too—
or it'll be the perfect revenge for the placemats and napkins
and dishes and fancy food and the beautification of my guest
room.

"When are we talking about?" she asks, her tone more
"firing squad" than "night under the stars."

"This Saturday and Sunday nights? I'll get someone to
cover for me Saturday so we can hike Saturday and be at the
site in time to pitch the tent by dark."

"Hike?" she demands. "Like, hike, hike? With a backpack?"

There might be a note of panic in her voice now. And I'm evil, because I'm enjoying it.

"Yeah. What'd you think I was talking about?"

"Car camping."

I shake my head in disgust. "That's not real camping."

"It felt pretty real to me the one time I did it."

"Oh, so you do do camping," I tease.

"I did camping, one horrible time."

"But if it was car camping you didn't do it right. So you don't know. You might love it."

She shakes her head, but her teeth clamp into her lower lip and I realize she's trying not to smile.

A feeling like laughter fills my chest.

This is how it is with us, so opposite you'd think we'd cancel each other out like matter and antimatter, but good, too.

Not good. Great.

Amazing.

26

LIV

I wake up feeling like I'm sleeping under a dentist's lead apron. My limbs are so heavy with satisfaction they don't want to move; my mind is so sluggish under layers of sleep I can barely string thoughts together.

Last night.

I almost purr with pleasure, remembering.

And then . . .

Shit! Didn't set alarm!

I open my eyes and it's almost 9:30. I was supposed to be up at 8:00 with Katie so Chase could go into the store.

I stagger downstairs and find Katie and Chase playing Candy Land on the kitchen table.

"Play with us!" Katie suggests. Or, actually, demands.

"She needs a cup of coffee," Chase tells her. He gets up from the table, crosses to the counter, and pours me a steaming cup. He hands it to me and I bring it close to my nose, the scent alone swoon-worthy. I suck down a few glorious hot sips and feel infinitely more human.

"Why are you still here? Why didn't you wake me up?"

"Thought you might need a little extra sleep," he says, smirking, eyes warm.

I go hot all over. "But—"

"Brooks can handle the store for a couple of hours. I thought you and Katie and I could go in together and you and Katie could get fitted for some hiking boots."

Oh. Right. Camping.

"Play Candy Land!" Katie exhorts.

"Let Liv drink her coffee and take her shower. I'll play with you."

"But I want her to play," Katie wails.

I brush her hair back from her face. "I'll play Chutes and Ladders with you later while Daddy's at work."

"How 'bout this," Chase says. "While Liv's showering, I'll tell you about something super fun I have planned for us. A camping trip! With Liv." Chase shoots me a look. Triumph.

Bastard! He knows he's sealed my fate. Telling Katie means there's no way I can back down. I won't break a five-year-old's heart, not even to avoid sleeping with bugs and dirt.

Katie's eyes are huge. "A camping trip? With a tent?"

"With a tent, and a cooking stove, and a special filter for making clean water . . ."

Even after I head upstairs for my shower, coffee mug in hand, I can still hear his voice behind me, listing the instruments of my torture.

SANDRA, a plump woman with curly gray hair who says she's worked in the store since before Chase took over, measures my foot. I didn't know people even did that anymore. I thought they just ordered three sizes from Zappos and chose the one that fit best.

Katie sits next to me, swinging her legs because they won't touch the floor. She stands, lining her foot up precisely when the saleswoman asks her to.

Sandra comes back with a stack of shoe boxes. She squats and helps Katie into a pair of cute pink hiking boots. Then she guides my feet into a pair of boots so brown, ugly, and stiff I'm not sure whether my desire to cry is more about loathing or pain. "Breaks your heart, doesn't it?" Sandra asks.

I look gratefully at her, thankful she's so sympathetic about the awful boots, then realize her question isn't about the boots, it's about Katie, who's hopping all over the store now, showing her boots to anyone who will look.

"Losing her mama like that," Sandra whispers.

"Yeah," I say quietly. Katie is better every day, but I know from personal experience that being motherless never really gets easier. All those times when someone else's mom brings cupcakes to class. When your friend skins a knee and you watch her mom cry with her over the sting of the alcohol. When you get your period.

Someday, when Katie's older, I'll tell her. You survive it, but you don't get over it.

"It's a terrible thing, no doubt about it," Sandra says briskly. "But then there's this other part of me that's—well, not glad, that's not what I mean at all; you don't ever wish ill of the dead—but at least now Chase'll get to be a real part of his daughter's life."

As if on cue, I hear Katie crowing with joy over her new

boots, and Chase chuckling, and I look over at them. My ovaries swell to bursting.

"You gotta give 'em a real try before you know if they're right for you," Sandra says, and my eyes fly to hers. She's looking at my feet.

Oh. The boots.

I obey the command, walking in the miserable boots back and forth. I'm distracted now, from the discomfort and the dislike. I stop in front of Sandra.

"Don't get me wrong," Sandra says. "I'm sorry Katie lost her mama. Nothing worse than that. But she has an amazing dad. And maybe a nice stepmama, someday, too?" Her voice rises, teasing.

She's talking about me. She thinks—

She thinks Chase and I—

And Katie—

What if…?

But there is no room in my life for what-ifs. There never has been, and there certainly isn't now.

"I'm just Katie's nanny. And only for another week."

"Oh!" Sandra blushes furiously. "I thought—I guess because of the shoes and the camping trip and the way you guys look at each other—"

She stammers to a stop, the sentence unfinished.

"How do you like those boots?" Sandra asks, recovering her equilibrium.

Relieved, I hold up a foot, which feels like it's been encased in concrete. "I hate them," I admit.

Sandra's smile widens. I think she's been messing with me. Maybe it's a test of some kind.

"Is there anything, I don't know—"

"Softer? Lighter weight?"

"Less like a ski boot?"

She opens another box and takes out a pair of boots I don't hate. I mean, I don't imagine they'll get a lot of use after the camping trip, but they don't make me want to curl up and rock, either. They're black and white, with craggy white soles and a diamond pattern in the nylon. I try them on and walk back and forth across the shoe area a few times, not exactly admiring them, but at least not hating them.

Sandra and I give them our joint stamp of approval, and I head over to find Chase and Katie.

Katie is playing with some of the bright-colored neck gaiters. "They're fairies," she says.

They do look a little bit like fairies.

"Where's your dad?"

"Helping a guy."

I round a corner to spot him chatting with a wiry dude. I hang back a ways, not wanting to interrupt.

"You'd be better off spending that money on a good wool base layer and a wool or fleece hat," Chase is telling him. "Your jacket may be twenty years old, but it's a good product and it's in good shape. Plus you're not going to be wearing it most of the time when you're hiking and sleeping, so the base layer will matter to you more. As long as the guys you're with aren't super status conscious. In which case, buy the new jacket."

The guy's laughing, and moving towards where Chase is directing him, and by the time Chase is done with him, he's thrown a new sleeping bag into the mix. Chase just has that way about him. He's trustworthy—because he's honest—and people know it. They want to buy from him.

I know he'll be able to convince Mike of that with his business plan.

As the guy heads for the checkout counter, Chase tells him, "Let me give you a business card for a guy who does trips up there." He hunts in his pockets and pulls one out.

The guy thanks him profusely, they exchange a manly handshake, and the guy strides off.

"Where's he going?" I ask.

"Alaska."

"Oh. Wow."

"Yup."

"You know people everywhere?"

"It turns out I kinda do," he says, grinning. He nods down at the box in my hand. "Nice boots. Those'll make you look like you like camping. They're magic boots."

I can't help my snort of laughter.

He takes the box from my hands and I follow him to the cash register, where he rings them up.

I hold out my credit card.

"Nope," he says.

"Oh, come on."

"I'm making you go camping. Supplies are on me."

There's a certain logic to that, and I don't fight him. "Thank you." I accept the box back from him.

"Hey," he says. "If you're done here, I have a plan. You game?"

"Do I get to know what the plan is?"

He shakes his head. "Nope. You just have to trust me."

"But I hate baseball," Liv whispers to me, being careful not to let Katie, in the back seat, overhear.

We've just pulled into a parking spot at Lake Lynn Park, where the single A Callalum Crows are playing their archrivals, the Grear Falls Divers.

"No, you only *think* you do, because you've never been to a minor league game." I slide out of my seat, shut the driver's side door, and open the back to free Katie from her harness.

As I straighten up, I confront Liv, who has rounded the car, forehead wrinkled.

"But I've been to a major league game, and aren't minor league games just bad major league games?"

I grin. "Nope. They're a totally different beast. You'll see."

With a small harumph, Liv falls in beside Katie and me, and we head into the park. We find our seats, which are in the second row on the first base line. Katie bounces up and down, thrilled. This is her first baseball game, but I've hyped her up about how close we are and how we're going to have hot dogs and Crackerjacks and ice cream, and she's bought the marketing, hook, line, and sinker.

Liv, on the other hand, is squinting at the field suspiciously.

"How did I let you rope me into this? There wasn't even a withheld orgasm involved." She murmurs this last, ostensibly for Katie's sake, but it also requires her to lean in close, her breath against my ear. My whole body responds to that faint ripple of touch. I want to pull her into my arms and kiss her, but this is *definitely* a family game.

"I told you to trust me, and you did," I point out.

"My first mistake," she says darkly.

"Stay with Katie?" I ask. "I'm getting us some food."

A few minutes later we're settled with beer (me), wine (her), hot dogs (all of us), and a big box of Crackerjacks. The game has started.

"The thing about minor league ball," I tell her, "is that anything can happen. In the major leagues, if you hit a fly ball into the outfield, someone is going to catch it. But in the minors?"

As if to illustrate my point, the batter—ours—powers one to right, and the fielder loses it in the sun. And Liv jumps to her feet and cheers.

Then she gives me a sheepish look and drops back into her seat. But too late.

"I saw that," I tell her.

"It was instinct," she says defensively.

"Uh-huh."

But as the game goes on, Liv gets more and more into it, pulling Katie to her feet to cheer with her. She claps with excitement when the crow mascot and the masked diver mascot do a three-legged race with fan partners, laughs and points and boosts Katie up to see better when the frisbee dogs come out. When two lucky kids get to do a wheelbarrow race with the mascots as their pilots, she hoots and howls her support for the crow team.

I just watch her, unable to hide my smile. Unable to keep the strange, buoyant feeling in my chest from threatening to carry me away.

And then it's the sixth inning and it's time for bubble wrestling.

Our mascot approaches our seats, and Katie jumps up, yelling, "Me! Me!"

"You," says the mascot, pointing in our direction—but not at Katie.

"No *way*," Liv says.

But the mascot has her by the hand and is pulling her up from her seat. Liv shoots me a pleading look, but I'm laughing so hard I can't help her out. Katie's laughing, too, and cheering for Liv.

They strap Liv into her bubble, along with the two other contestants, also women, and the three of them bounce off each other a few times to delighted cheers from the crowd.

The people cheering the loudest are definitely Katie and me, especially when Liv is declared the victor. They liberate her from her bubble and she trots back to us, fist in the air, face lit with joy.

"Oh my God, that was so fun!"

"Livvy Livvy Livvy!" Katie crows. "You winned! You winned the bubbles!" She catapults herself at Liv, and Liv throws her arms around both of us and kisses us both, first Katie on the forehead, then me on the mouth. Of all the kisses we've exchanged this one is the most chaste, and yet this is the moment I want to freeze.

"Daddy!" Katie says. "I love baseball!"

We sit back in our seats. I sneak a glance at Liv, who's beaming, glowing. Nothing secret about her joy right now, and for some reason, that's even better than the secret sexy smile.

I reach over Katie and take her hand. In the seconds before our fingers touch, I regret the impulse, sure she's going to yank her hand away.

But she doesn't. Instead, she twines her fingers into mine, holding tight.

We sit like that for the rest of the game, our fingers linked across Katie's lap, and I don't let myself think about anything outside the bubble that holds the three of us for this short and perfect moment.

28

LIV

"Are you okay?" I ask, concerned.

Katie's asleep, wiped out from the baseball game this afternoon, and Chase is lying on his back on the living room floor, his eyes fixed on the ceiling.

"Yeah," he says. "I'm thinking."

"It looks like it hurts."

I sink to the floor next to him. I want to touch the rumpled mess of his soft hair, the strong planes of chest and stomach, and the strip of bare, pale skin between his t-shirt and jeans, including a tease of happy trail that I wouldn't mind following up a mountain.

But I keep my hands—and mouth—to myself for the moment, because he really does look like his mind is somewhere else completely.

Besides, this afternoon scared me a little. I had such a good time. But more than that, when Chase reached out and held my hand, it felt like there was something going on—something more than just friends with really great benefits.

And I can't wrap my mind around that.

I need to keep it—my mind—clear, so I can do what I need to do. Earn the money for this temporary gig, buy a new car, and hit the road.

Chase closes one eye and wrinkles up his face.

"I had a really great conversation with Brooks' and Sawyer's friend Gabe, who runs an outdoor adventuring business near Bend, Oregon. And he loved the idea of partnering with the store somehow. He said to get him a proposal and he'll take a look. So now I'm working on that, too. Trying to figure out what I could offer him. I'm thinking about building the online site so his customers—or any partner's customers—could access an exclusive area and choose items geared specifically for the trip they're taking."

"Ooh, that sounds great. What if," I say slowly, thinking aloud, "you did branded merchandise? What's Gabe's company's name?"

"Wilder Adventures," Chase says.

"Okay, so what if you did base layers and Ts and stuff with the Wilder logo on them, in addition to whatever your regular offerings are."

I can see his mind spinning a million miles per hours on that.

"That could totally work," he says.

I notice, for the first time, that he's surrounded by a blizzard of 8.5 x 11 sheets. Apparently Chase has never heard of a spiral notebook.

"Would it be helpful if I typed some of this into a doc? Just so it's not all on paper?"

He looks up at me, and I'm used to lots of things about Chase, but not the look of outright gratitude he's wearing now.

"You wouldn't mind?"

"Hell, no," I say. I go and get my laptop and sit back down on the floor next to him.

He flips onto his stomach, sprawled out like a little kid, and writes furiously on a piece of paper. His handwriting is borderline illegible and his spelling is atrocious—I completely understand now how he was a near-disaster in school as a kid. But there's nothing wrong with his business logic. He thinks fast and even if ninety percent of the population might not be able to make any sense of his shorthand, we're somehow perfectly in tune tonight, him dashing stuff down as fast as it comes to him and me translating it into more readable form. We bounce ideas off each other like I bounced off the other bubbles today on the field.

It's fun working with him like this. I love the way our minds add up to more than the sum of their parts.

Chase makes a humming noise that draws my gaze. A lock of hair has fallen over his forehead and there are lines of concentration etched deep. He scribbles, rests the end of his pencil against his lips, scribbles again. Smiles, so that the lines vanish from his brow. Something expands and contracts in my chest, generous, then sharp.

He looks up, catching my eye, and time freezes.

He sets the pencil aside, crawls across the floor to where I'm sitting on the couch, takes the laptop off my lap, and sets it down on the coffee table.

"All work and no play . . ." he says, his voice rough. He kneels up between my legs and I twine my arms around his neck. I can smell his skin, so clean and specific it makes my mouth water and my fingers curl. It takes forever for his mouth to meet mine.

"Chase," I murmur. There are things I want to ask him, but I don't know what they are. There are things I want to tell him, but I don't know what they are, either. I feel languid and urgent at the same time, like honey and buzzing bees.

He only touches his mouth to mine. "Mmm," he says. "I love the way you taste."

"I love the way you taste, too."

He kisses me again, this kiss a little longer, a little more complete. I want his tongue in my mouth. I want his hands on my breasts. I want—

"I like kissing you more than I've ever liked kissing anyone," he says.

My heart pauses.

"Me too," I manage. But I feel such a mix of things. Such a rush of lust I can barely keep it inside my skin. So much impatience.

And also the feeling of teetering, like I'm balanced somewhere precarious and might fall at any moment.

L iv pulls back, and an expression flits across her face as she pulls the laptop back onto her lap, like a shield.

I think I might know what that expression is about, because I feel it, too. Something is happening here that neither of us was planning, and that neither of us knows what to do about. Her hand in mine at the baseball game. The way it felt just now to work together on something so important to me.

And I meant what I said about kissing her. Like nothing else I've ever felt. Like there's a layer to physical sensation I never knew existed.

It's so good, and also pretty fucking scary.

Because for the first time, I want to ask her to stay.

As soon as I let myself have the thought, I flash back on when I asked Thea to stay.

Don't go. I love you. And I know, if you give me the chance, I can make you happy.

It was hard to get the words out; it felt like they were

being forced through a too-small tube; it hurt my chest. But it felt good, too; they came out on a wave of hope that lasted about as long as it took for Thea's expression to change. Her face—even her body language—went very still.

Thea said, *I've thought about this a lot, Chase. We're too different. I know they say opposites attract, but that's just bullshit that people use to comfort themselves. Even if I told myself I wouldn't, I'd always be wanting you to be different. I'd be waiting for you to catch up, to polish up, clean up, be smoother and suaver. We'd go to parties and I'd feel you next to me, rough around the edges, and I wouldn't think we complement each other so well; I'd want to buff the roughness off. Make you someone you aren't. And —it wouldn't be fair to you, and it wouldn't be fun for me.*

"Chase?"

Liv is peering at me, concerned.

"Sorry. Thinking of something else."

Fuck Thea, right? I mean, fuck her. Fuck her moral superiority and her judgment and her smooth is better than rough. The world is full of beautiful rough things—the Grand Canyon, studded snow tires, tree bark, the Cascade range, all jagged and uncivilized and wonderful.

But even setting Thea aside, I can't just ask Liv to stay, not right now, not like this. Not after she told me how twitchy and awful it feels to be trapped. I need to get her to a place where it feels possible for her.

Instead, I tell her, "We should have a party. Invite a few of my friends, a few of yours."

"Like a going-away party?"

"Yeah," I say. "A going-away party."

"That would be fun."

She sounds like she means it. She doesn't look like the

idea of going away gives her pause. So it's like I thought. I have to give her a little more time. I have to give both of us a little more time to figure out how it all fits together. We'll have the party, and we'll have the camping trip.

Surely by the end of the camping trip...

I realize something in that moment. How much weight I'm putting on this camping trip in my head.

I didn't ask Liv to go camping with me to help me with Katie or to tease or torture her. I asked her to go because if I can make her fall in love with camping, maybe I can make her fall in love with me.

That's all I've got; that's the whole of my plan.

I'm going to take her into the woods and show her all the things I love the most so she can learn to love things she thought she couldn't.

I hope.

C hase and I can't agree on anything about "our" barbecue.

Obviously, there are certain things we can agree on. Burgers. Dogs. Buns. Relish, ketchup, mustard. Corn.

Where we differ is on, well, everything else.

Like salads.

"Potato salad. And maybe coleslaw."

I push a recipe across the table to him.

He makes a face. "How do you even say that word?"

"Nee-swaz."

"What is that, French?"

I show him a couple of others.

"Tortellini with ham, red onion, and pesto? Whatever happened to classic macaroni salad, you know, with carrots, drowning in mayo?"

"If I'm doing the cooking, what do you care?"

"I care if you serve food whose name I can't pronounce."

Tablecloths turn out, also, to be an issue.

"It's a picnic table, Liv."

"It would look really nice with something bright colored draped over it, and a few tea lights in glass bowls or squares."

"My friends will laugh their asses off."

"Sandra will not laugh her ass off. Camilla will not laugh her ass off. Eve will not laugh her ass off."

He rolls his eyes.

We fight about drinks.

"Beer. Beer is all you need."

He sings a few bars of it to the tune of Love is all you need . . .

"Beer is not all you need. We should have wine and something sparkly and nonalcoholic . . ."

And Thursday night, ten minutes before our first guests show up, we fight about the music.

"No. No fucking way."

Katie, obviously, is not on the patio with us.

"It's good background music."

"No jazz."

"What do you have against jazz?"

"That it sucks," Chase says.

"You can't damn a whole genre like that. Maybe there's some you would like, if you gave it a chance."

Chase raises both eyebrows at me. "Maybe," he says. "But I'm sure as hell not going to do my research at the expense of my closest friends."

I let Chase win that round, which is how our picnic comes to be backgrounded by classic rock and '80s and '90s hits.

We have agreed on nothing, and yet, when the party

starts, through some strange alchemy, it is seamless and fantastic.

Our guests drink and talk, mingling and chowing and chatting. Chase and I move among them, refilling drinks, replenishing food, flipping meat on the grill, chatting up each other's friends.

It's past dusk, now, and candles glow on every surface I could stash them on, illuminating smiles and bright eyes. There's a sweet tidal wash of conversation and laughter. Katie and her friend race off to play complicated games out of sight, then return, mingling at thigh height, charming adults into giving them food and drink. When she passes me, I bend down to ask if she's having a good time.

She nods vehemently.

"What's the best part?"

"The woot beer," she says, with a big smile.

"How much root beer have you had?"

"Four cups."

I close my eyes. "Who poured it for you?"

"Daddy!"

I'm not sure whether she's answering my question or greeting the man who is suddenly standing at my side.

"Great party."

He's wearing cargo shorts and leather sandals and a T-shirt that says Just another beer drinker with a camping problem and he's got a beer in one hand. He looks maddeningly sexy. It's the wine. Alcohol always makes me loose and a little warm, and the instant Chase stepped into my personal space, I got a few degrees warmer—and tinglier.

"We did good," he says.

"It was the salads." I fight to keep the smile off my lips.

"It was the classic rock."

Faced off, feigning dead seriousness, we both begin to laugh.

"What's so funny, Daddy?" Katie asks.

I'm about to try to explain the joke to a five-year-old when he says, "I like Liv."

He says it with no particular significance—not, definitely, the way middle school girls say like—but my heart speeds up anyway, and I glance nervously at his face, but he's looking at Katie, his gaze rich with affection.

Damn the wine—it's making me paranoid. The last thing I need is anyone getting in over their head here.

I mean, I'm in a little bit over my head already. I'm in deeper with Chase than I ever meant to be. I almost think, if I let myself, I could fall for him. But I'm still clear with myself that I'm not going there again, or at least not with a guy who has a pre-existing anti-commitment condition.

"I like Liv, too," says Katie.

Brooks saunters up. He's a head taller than Chase, with lots of shaggy brown hair and a full beard—very mountain man. "I'm Brooks. I think we've met once? Or maybe I just ogled you from afar. Great party."

"Thanks, I think," I say, laughing.

"Those salads are fu—"

We both look down at Katie.

"—awesome."

"Why, thank you, Brooks." I give Chase a long, hard look, and he holds his palms out in surrender.

Brooks looks confused.

"The salads were a tough sell for Chase," I explain. "As

were the candles, the tablecloths, the wine, the sparkling juice—"

"Just be glad I didn't let her pick the music," Chase says.

"The music is the best part," Brooks says.

"You see?" Chase demands.

"Liv, important question for you," Brooks says, oblivious to all of it. "Who is the woman sitting at the end of the picnic table?"

"That's my friend Eve." I'm used to answering that question. Guys always go after Eve, who is five eight and is built like a model—the bathing suit kind, not the bony kind that looks best draped in a cabled sweater.

"Ah."

"Do you need an introduction?"

"No," Brooks says. "I just need to know that you won't kill me if I go home with her tonight."

"No, but *I* might kill you if you get me in trouble by association," Chase puts in.

I laugh. "Eve can take care of herself."

That's an understatement. Eve never wants to get married and doesn't do relationships. Her parents made each other miserable, and after they divorced, Eve's mom and stepdad made each other miserable, and Eve's dad and stepmom made each other miserable, and her dad is currently making Eve's second stepmom miserable... so yeah, Eve has opted out. She prides herself on having sex like a man: "no regrets, no repeats." I'd warn Brooks—but based on what Chase has told me about him, Brooks follows the same motto.

"Excellent news," Brooks says, his face lighting up. "See you later, then." And off he goes, a moment later at Eve's side, whispering something in her ear that I can see—even from this distance—makes her smile.

"Huh," Chase says. "That should be . . . interesting."

"How so?"

"Like, irresistible force meets immovable object."

"I was thinking more like two people clad in giant plastic bubbles. Big bump, and then off in totally different directions."

"Matter and antimatter?" he suggests.

"Only if by that you mean there will be nothing left afterward to suggest anything happened."

I have barely gotten the words out when a vast quantity of honey-colored hair—enough to merit its own zip code—suddenly appears in my peripheral vision.

"Liv! This is the best party ever! And can I please, please, please, please have the recipe for the pesto salad?"

It's Eve. "You see?" I say to Chase. "They love the salads."

He rolls his eyes and drifts away as I start listing the ingredients in my salad to Eve.

As soon as he's gone, she grabs my arm. "Liv! What's going on with you two?"

"What do you mean?"

She rolls her eyes at the transparency of my evasion. "You can't fool me."

Eve waits patiently, until I can't stand the silence. "Okay. Yes. Things have . . . um, happened. And it's—" I grope for words and fail. I close my eyes, swoon-style.

She raises one perfectly curved, salon-tweezed eyebrow. "Really."

"Yeah. But it's just that. Friends with benefits. We talked

about it. We agreed. It's really not a big deal. Riding the coaster."

Eve raises her eyebrows. "Mmm-hmm."

I punch her arm. "It is. Speaking of which, Brooks?"

She looks in his direction. He looks back, smiling, one eyebrow raised.

"I might take that for a spin later," she says, grinning at him and then at me. "But we're not talking about me. We're talking about you. So, just sex and barbecues? And then you go to Golden, and that's it?"

"We're going camping this weekend, and then, yeah, I leave."

"Camping?"

I wouldn't have thought it was possible, but her eyebrows creep even higher.

"Eve, quit it. It's not like that."

"But maybe it could be," she says quietly.

"He's so not that guy."

"What guy?" Eve asks. She touches my shoulder, her eyes gentle.

I shake my head.

"The kind who could tell you he wants you forever, and actually mean it?"

All I can do is nod. I'm too choked up to talk.

"Are you sure?"

31

CHASE

Later in the party, I escape to the edge of the yard and stand, nursing my beer. I'm tired of doing the polite host gig, and all the small talk, and I just want to watch for a few minutes. So I do. I watch Katie, playing some elaborate make-believe game with her friend Ju, and it already feels hard to imagine a time when she wasn't in my life every day. I watch Brooks chat up Eve, the two of them leaning in toward each other, faces bright. I watch Rodro say something to his wife that makes her blush. There's a lot of sex in the air. You can feel the charge. Or maybe it's just me. This week, I feel like I'm constantly on simmer.

Mostly, though, I'm watching Liv. She's wearing a red dress covered with daisies and black sandals with straps that criss-and-cross her ankles and make me want to peel them away.

I wonder what she's wearing underneath her dress.

Simmer to boil in two seconds flat. Now that I know what she smells and tastes and sounds like, what her face looks like when she comes, I'm obsessed.

"She's amazing, right?"

It's Eve. She's come up beside me, a glass of wine in her hand, and her eyes are on Liv, too.

"I'm going to miss her so much when she goes."

She says it casually, but I know there's subtext. She's baiting me. I don't say anything.

"Chase. Can I give you some advice?"

"Do I have a choice?"

Eve laughs. I've only met Eve a couple of times, but she's a real straight shooter.

"She's more complicated than she seems. She's very tough, which I think you know. But she's also—I hate it when people say broken, so I won't say it. Healing. She's healing. Five foster families in eleven years, and they were good people, but nothing stuck . . ."

"Yeah. She told me."

"Ever noticed how when she talks about them, she ticks them off on her fingers? Like it's the only way she can remember all of them?" She demonstrates, counting off on her fingers. "And she's still moving around. Two different colleges, jumping from house to house in her nanny job. Can I ask you something?"

I nod.

"Has she ever mentioned Zeke?" She watches my face carefully. "You don't know that story, huh? Ask her. Just—" She holds up a finger. "Brace yourself. You'll want to rip his guts out afterward. I just think you should know the whole big picture, before—"

She turns and looks at me. Eve has these dark-gold eyes, eerie. They look like they can see right through you. Through me. And maybe she can, because she says, "—before someone gets hurt."

It wasn't what I thought she was going to say.

"I'm not going to hurt her."

My eyes find Liv again, kneeling to hug Katie, kissing Katie's head, her copper-penny hair bright against Katie's gold, and my chest splits down the middle at the sight of them together. Damn it, I was never going to do this again.

I turn back to find Eve watching me. And I suddenly understand what she's trying to say.

"You're not worried I'm going to hurt her, are you?" I ask.

She shakes her head.

"You're worried she's going to hurt me."

"She won't do it on purpose," she says, quietly. "It's just—when you've never really had a place to call your own, it can be hard to stay put. And you want to ask her to, don't you?"

I think about lying to her, but Eve, like my guy friends, seems like the kind of person who will suss out a lie in seconds flat. Her eyes are on me, soft and sympathetic.

"You don't think she'll stay. Even if I ask."

She watches Liv, who has taken both Katie's hands and is dancing her around to Journey's "Any Way You Want It." Then she turns back to me, those pale brown eyes steady on mine.

"I think if anyone could make her want to stay, it would be you."

I sit bolt upright in bed.

Katie's crying.

I drag myself from the bed—mine, because Chase and I have been careful not to let Katie catch us sleeping in the same bed—pull a hoodie around me, and hurry down the hall.

Her door is open a little ways, and as I get closer, I hear something that stops me in my tracks. A second voice, interwoven with Katie's still-panicked cries. Chase's, deep and husky from sleep.

I stand in the shadows of the hall, listening. I can't hear his words, only the rhythm and texture of them, soft and soothing. A sound you can wrap yourself in, and that's what I do. I lean against the wall and wrap myself in the sound of Chase.

Katie's voice quiets, more and more intermittent until I don't hear her at all. Now I can only hear Chase's voice.

What he's murmuring, over and over again, is *I love you.*

If I were not me, and he were not him, and I were not

leaving, I think it would be incredibly easy to fall in love with him.

The thing I'm learning is that there is a lot of Chase that no one knows. Everyone knows bits and pieces. But maybe now I know the most bits and pieces. And they add up to so much more than I'd thought. To this amazing man, with so many dimensions, who has worked hard to be the best person he can be, despite the forces arrayed against him.

"Jesus, Liv!" Chase says, emerging from Katie's room and jumping a foot, startling me out of my reverie.

He's wearing nothing but pajama pants. It's a good look for him.

"Sorry. I didn't mean to startle you. I was just thinking. She was wrong. Thea."

"What?"

"She was wrong to try to keep Katie from you. You're a great dad. The best."

He looks pleased. And embarrassed. He shrugs me off.

"Liv?" he asks.

"Mmm-hmm."

"Who's Zeke?"

My stomach lurches. "How do you know about Zeke?"

"Eve said I should ask you."

Irritation twists in my stomach. Giving him too much power again. I wish she hadn't.

"He's an asshole guy I dated a long time ago. He's no one."

"Well, if it's no big deal," he says lightly, "then you shouldn't mind telling me about him."

He takes my hand and leads me away from Katie's room, down the hall and into his room. We stop inside the door. "Shoot," he says.

I shrug. "Seriously. It's nothing. I dated him after college. We moved in together. Pretty soon after that, I caught him kissing someone else. You see? Classic story of an asshole."

"Were you in love with him?"

It is the last, the very last, question I was expecting Chase to ask. I hesitate, then nod.

"A little? Or a lot?"

"What does it matter?"

"It matters."

I turn away. There's a crack in the hallway paint that looks like the letter J.

"Liv."

My chest is tight. "A lot. Way too fucking much."

"And you thought he loved you back?"

I pull the hoodie around me and cross my arms.

"He knew about my mom and that I'd grown up in foster care."

I'm not sure why those words decided to come out of my mouth right then. Or the next ones:

"And that I never got to stay anywhere."

I have the choky sensation of tears rising in my throat, behind my eyes, but I battle them back. I will not give him the satisfaction.

"What happened?" Chase asks quietly. "What did he do to you?"

His voice is steely. I think maybe if Zeke were here, Chase would hurt him. And I like that, just a little.

"The night he asked me to move in with him, I'd woken up with a nightmare. It didn't happen a lot anymore, but sometimes. It had happened a few times when he was there. This time, he held me, and then he asked me to move in with him. He said, 'That way, I'll always be here. You'll never have to wake up alone again.'"

My voice is shaking.

"You know what makes me the maddest? I'd known better for years. It's not that people are bad. They're not bad, they're just weak. They can't keep their promises. They change their minds, they fall off the wagon, they give in to temptation, they get themselves arrested, they fall for someone cuter, younger, sweeter—whatever. But you're an idiot if you think otherwise. That's the thing. You're an idiot if you think otherwise. I was an idiot."

"Not all people."

"All. People."

"Liv, that's not true."

"All people make mistakes. All people are fallible."

"Yes, but that doesn't mean—"

I talk over him. "He owned a small house, and I moved in there with him, and I remember when I was decorating, I remember thinking, *This is it. I'm doing this for real this time. Permanent.* I didn't have to think about how I'd dismantle it for moving, or any of that."

Chase looks stricken. "Liv."

"It's okay. I want to tell you the rest. Pretty soon after that —six weeks? Eight weeks?—I went to his office to surprise him with lunch and caught him kissing—like, passionately kissing—one of his coworkers. The worst part—I know this is crazy, but I swear, it's true—the worst part was packing up my things. Not because the house was anything special, but because I'd been dumb enough to think it was mine."

He's never taken his eyes off my face the whole time I'm

talking. Now he says, "You weren't an idiot. You're not an idiot. Trusting people doesn't make you stupid."

He puts one big, warm hand on my hair, slides it down around my jaw, and even though he's wrong, I don't argue. I lean into his touch. He brings his other hand up and pushes my hoodie off my shoulders. He pulls me into his arms. It feels unbelievably good, the heat of his bare torso soaking straight through my thin pajamas.

He picks me up so both my legs are around his waist and carries me to the bed. He lowers me gently into it.

I think he wants to make love. And I would. My body is blooming warm and ready for him, just from the care in his touch and the press of his body.

But that's not what happens.

What happens is better.

He crawls into the bed beside me. He wraps his arms around me and pulls me close. The wall of muscle is there. The feel of his breath against my hair. The throb of his heart, a steady, sure rhythm, like the murmur of his voice to Katie earlier.

He holds me, just like that, arms never loosening their hold, until the tension goes out of my limbs and I fall into sleep.

Chase is pawing through my things. "No," he says, setting aside two pairs of jeans. "No jeans. And what's this? Three bras? Why three bras?"

"Two changes, and one in case I fall in the lake."

"In case you—what?"

"That's what my first foster mom used to say. One extra in case you fall in the lake."

"Liv," he says sternly. "You're carrying everything in that backpack." He gestures. "You can't take anything extra. Not even underwear. If you fall in the lake you will hang up your clothes to dry out."

"I told you I don't know anything about camping!"

"And what are these?" He holds up a pair of socks.

"Socks."

"I should have known," he says, shaking his head as if I am far beyond help. "I should have known that if you didn't have any decent shoes, you wouldn't have any decent socks."

He leaves the room and comes back with two pairs of ugly

brown thick wool socks. "These. Now. What about hiking pants?"

"Chase." It is my turn to be utterly scornful. "Look at me. Do you think I own hiking pants?"

He rolls his eyes. "I should have made you do this inventory before we went to the store the other day. Athletic pants are fine. Or leggings, whatever—something lightweight and flexible. Just not jeans."

"My jeans are flexible and lightweight," I argue, but he gives me a look that shuts me up.

He holds up my warmest sweater, a cotton cardigan, and shakes his head to convey his despair. He leaves again, then comes back with a wool sweater that he thrusts into my hands. It's rough gray color-flecked wool and when I take it from him, I smell lanolin, Chase's spicy deodorant, and his skin.

Which makes me want to drop the whole packing project and nibble my way from Chase's collarbone to his ear and then along the rough, stubbled edge of his gorgeous jaw to his unbelievably talented mouth.

He's watching me right now, hunger in his eyes. As if we haven't done it ten times in the last five days.

Not last night, though. Last night, he just held me.

Something clenches in my chest, painful and needy.

In the next room, Katie is playing. Occasionally we hear her voice rise as one of the parent dolls in the dollhouse gets strict with one of the child dolls. One of the parents is a daddy.

The other is a nanny.

It makes me want to cry, and also to snatch Katie up in a fierce hug.

My emotions are like unruly children today.

I realize I'm still standing there holding the sweater, and I laugh.

"What?"

"Who needs a wool sweater in July? That's not exactly packing light, is it?"

"Take my word for it, you will not regret packing a wool sweater."

"It's hot right now."

It is, unseasonably for the Seattle area.

"Liv. Just do what I say, okay? And we'll both live to tell the tale."

Right now, I'd do pretty much anything he said, which scares the crap out of me.

He finishes criticizing my packing choices, and then we move on to the actual packing. He lines my pack with a garbage bag first.

"What's that for?"

"In case it rains."

"We won't go if it rains, will we?"

He doesn't dignify that with an answer. He begins rolling my clothes and stuffing them into the backpack. He throws in an assortment of objects, identifying them as group gear. Some are familiar, like a first aid kid, a plastic plate, and a fork. Others are mysterious—a red canister, a small black bag, a ziplock with—

"Is that toilet paper?"

He nods.

"We have to bring our own toilet paper?"

He closes his eyes.

"Chase! What is the orange trowel for?"

"For digging holes."

"Why do we have to dig holes?"

He opens his mouth to say something—I have no idea what—when his phone rings.

"Chase," he says, and listens. Then, "Oh, Emily. Oh, God, I forgot. Yes . . . No . . . I . . . I was going to take her camping, but . . ."

Does this mean I am going to be reprieved? Because that would be spectacular.

There's a long pause, and I watch Chase's face, the spasm of the muscle at his jaw, the set of his mouth.

"I think she would like that. I think she would like it very much. I think—I think I should check with her first, but—"

He listens, and his eyes find mine, full of grief.

"I'll—I'll call you back, but if there's any way, yes, of course, of course we'll get her to you."

He gets off the phone, and turns a look on me that—well, it stops me cold. It's so shattered.

"Shit. That was Emily. Oh, shit." He paces.

"What?"

Turned away from me, staring at the far wall, he says, "It's Thea's birthday weekend. I'd actually forgotten. I can't believe I forgot. She asked if she could see Katie, if she could take Katie overnight . . ." He puts both his hands on the wall. "Fuck. You should have heard her. You've met her, she's this dour Scandinavian—and here she is, crying, telling me she'll take Katie to the zoo, to the aquarium, out for ice cream, anything Katie wants. Begging. She said—"

He closes his eyes.

"She said, 'I just want to see my little girl.'"

My throat gets tight. "Oh, shit."

I cross the room to him, put my hand in the middle of his back. The heat soaks into my palm. I place the other hand beside it, slide them around his sides until I'm hugging him, my front to his back. He doesn't turn to hug me back, but slowly, his breathing eases and his body relaxes, and that makes me feel like the champion of the world.

"I have to bring her."

I nod against his back.

"But she's going to be so upset about the camping."

"No, she'll be fine. Here's what you do. You present it to Katie like it's the most exciting news in the world. 'Grandma wants you to come have a sleepover at her house! She wants to take you to the zoo! And the aquarium! Do you want to go?'"

His face brightens. He nods. "Okay. Yeah. She'll totally want to."

"You don't even mention the camping. She's young enough that she might not even realize that one activity is happening in place of the other. But if she brings it up, you say, 'We can go camping next weekend!'"

"But you won't be here."

Right. Because I'll be gone.

I've been trying not to think about that too much. Because what started out originally as the perfect end point to our extracurriculars is approaching way too fast.

Meanwhile, I should be thrilled, because now I don't have to go camping.

I release Chase and start removing my clothes from the backpack where he's stuffed them.

"What are you doing?"

"Unpacking?"

"Why?"

"Because we're not going camping."

He crosses his arms. "I didn't say that. I said I'd go again with Katie next weekend."

I stare at him.

"Liv, you can't bail on me now. We're almost completely packed. Half the group gear is in your pack. I've been looking forward to this all week."

"To torturing me."

"Maybe a little," he admits. "You bought candles and dishes. And placemats. You turned my guest room into—a work of art."

I can tell he doesn't mean that as a compliment, which, sadly, makes me smile.

"And anyway, it's not just to torture you. It's to hang out with you. Hanging out around the campfire isn't that different from watching movies together."

"Minus the toilet, the warm bed, the electronics, the hair dryer, and all the other trappings of civilization."

He makes a face. "Civilization is overrated."

"I think it's underrated."

His brows draw together. "Let me ask you this. Why did you do it? Why did you buy the placemats and make the nice dinner? Why did you redo the guest room? Did you do it to torture me?"

I don't have to think too hard about the answer. "Of course not. I did it because it was important to me. Beautiful things are important to me."

He nods, as if that makes perfect sense. "That's how the woods are for me. Important. And I want to show you why."

I open my mouth to protest, to say that he can tell me why, he doesn't need to show me.

"Also," he says, quickly, "I'll make you s'mores with really good dark chocolate and then we can go skinny-dipping and I can spread you out on your sleeping bag in front of a blazing fire and eat you out in view of the sky and God and the whole world, while the cool breeze makes your nipples hard."

I'm honestly not sure if it's the marshmallows and oozing chocolate or how hard my nipples now are, but I'm a goner.

"Chase, I hate you."

"I know, babe. I hate you, too."

He doesn't say it like he means it, though. He says it like he means the exact opposite. And for a moment, not even a whole second, I wish he did, and then I stop, because—

Because he's him and I'm me and I'm leaving.

It's my mantra now. It would be so damn easy to forget.

He says, "So you'll still go with me this weekend?"

"Fuck you," I tell him, but we both know I'm going camping with him.

Because Chase possesses the ability to convince even the smartest girls to leave their in-case-you-fall-in-the-lake panties at home.

34

CHASE

We're a couple hundred feet into the woods and already I'm feeling like a whole new man.

Nothing else is like this.

I love the forest. The way everything hovers dark and close, sun filtering down like it's been tossed in handfuls. The trees are older than the Constitution, their trunks bigger around than I can wrap my arms, fuzzy with lichen and moss. Overhead, the treetops spear patches of blue sky, and you get dizzy from the sensation of falling upward. And there are the smells. Leaves and needles and hardwood and loamy dirt and life and decay.

Also, Liv's hair is in a ponytail. A high ponytail, which, if anyone's polling, is the sexiest kind.

I watch it swing behind her as she walks, long and thick and the color of copper.

I am so going to wrap that ponytail around my hand later and hold her head still while I kiss her and fuck her.

The thought makes me want to whistle.

Ahead of me, Liv pauses.

"You okay?"

"Is it supposed to hurt?"

"What hurts?"

"My shoulders."

"It's going to hurt a little. Because we didn't train ahead of time and you're carrying almost forty pounds."

Despite my best efforts, I couldn't get her pack any lighter than that. She insisted on a few things I knew she wouldn't care about in the end, like having her own toothpaste and her own deodorant. And a mini bottle of shampoo in case—

In case what? I demanded.

I don't know. In case there's a shower.

I didn't laugh, and I didn't try to talk her out of it. Sometimes you need a security blanket. Fathering a five year old has taught me a lot of good life lessons like that.

"Here, hang on," I tell her. I lift the pack from the top and tighten her waist strap a little. Then the chest compression strap.

"You just like the way it makes my boobs look."

"Not gonna argue with that."

But I'm not actually looking at her tits. I'm looking at her face. I'm standing so close to her, and suddenly it occurs to me: she's not wearing makeup.

I'm not sure I've ever seen her without makeup before. Not even in the middle of the night.

Her eyelashes are a pale blond flutter, her skin is pale and creamy, her eyelids almost translucent. She is delicate and vulnerable and incredibly beautiful. So beautiful it makes my throat hurt.

I look away, yanking on her shoulder strap to shorten it. "Better?"

"Oh, yeah, lots better."

"Most of the weight's supposed to be on your hips and chest, not your shoulders."

We hike on. One foot in front of the other. The perfect meditation.

We stop for lunch and lean our packs against a boulder beside a stream. The sky is blue, the stream glints in the sun, burbling as it runs over the rocks. It's like something out of a storybook.

I pull food out. I take it from her pack, to lighten her up as best I can. We're doing pitas and peanut butter. Oh, and oranges. If I can, I like fresh fruit the first day.

"It's not gourmet," I say, feeling unusually apologetic.

The corner of her mouth tips up. "I was hoping for a vichyssoise starter course."

"I don't even know what that is."

"I know—that's why I said it."

She eats, though, with gusto, which is one of those things camping does for you. Makes you hungry.

I watch her lick the last of her peanut butter off the plastic knife. I must make an unintentional, appreciative sound, because she gives me another of those sexy half-smiles and licks more thoroughly. I narrow my eyes at her.

"Be careful," I warn. "Or you will get taken over the top of this rock."

She eyes it.

"I'm not kidding."

"I'm not refusing."

I yank her toward me and kiss her, licking into her mouth the way she was going at that knife, until she moans and clutches my shirt. Then I release her. We both know it's not going to happen here. We're still too close to the trail entrance and only a couple of yards off the main trail. Later today, we'll take a less-traveled side trail to a lake I know, and then we'll make camp and—

"Have you ever had sex in the woods?"

Apparently she boarded the same thought train I did. I am such a fan of Liv's dirty mind, I can't even. I shake my head.

"Really?" She is obviously delighted. "I'm your first! I'm not your first anything!"

You're the first woman since Thea who—

—I care about, is how I finish the thought. I'm not sure why it feels so much like if I use the word love, there's no going back. No way to keep from being hurt if she can't love what I love.

If she can't love who I am.

If she tells me we're too different.

If she tells me she'll always need me to change.

If she won't stay.

"Woods blow job?" she asks, eyebrows high.

"Nope."

"Hand job?"

"If we go back to high school and college, yeah. Also, a lotta cars parked at the edge of the woods, but that's different."

"Yeah, no, that doesn't count. Oooh. This is going to be fun."

I don't say, 'I told you so,' but I'm thinking it.

Another couple of miles in—when we realized we wouldn't have Katie, I planned a longer hike—she stops and I nearly crash into her.

"I need the . . . um, facilities."

I dig out the ziplock bag with the TP and trowel and hand them to her.

"Leave no trace," I say.

She scowls. "I hate you."

"So you've said."

She disappears, returning a few minutes later with a dark expression on her face.

"For my going-away present, you're taking me to the fanciest restaurant in Seattle."

I groan, loudly.

And am grateful she's walking ahead of me and can't see me grinning.

35

LIV

"I'm dead," I wail. A few minutes ago we left the main trail, and now we are delving deep down a narrow side trail that seems to be getting more and more overgrown. Every part of my entire body hurts. I think I'd probably be crying, except there is no water left in my body. All of it has been excreted as sweat that has pooled between my backpack and my back.

"We have less than a mile to go."

"I can't."

"You can. I guarantee it."

"My feet are killing me. My hips are killing me. My shoulders are killing me. My neck is killing me."

"Here. Try this. It's an old chant, maybe army. It's supposed to distract you and give you a rhythm. 'Left. Left. Left my wife and forty-eight kids, right—'"

My steps are backwards from his counting, and I almost trip over myself, my feet are so leaden. "It didn't work out. I was on my left."

"Just put one foot in front of the other."

I'm about to protest that I can't, but it's impossible to miss the logic of his command. We are in the middle of nowhere, in the middle of the wilderness, and we've already hiked something like six miles. There's no going back. Only forward.

Chase resumes the chant. "'Right. Right. Right in the middle of the kitchen floor. Left. Left . . .'"

It's more like stumbling than walking at this point, each step an act of faith that my foot will actually catch me. And somehow we keep moving forward, and then we emerge into a clearing and—

"Oh. Wow."

There's a small rocky beach and a crystal-blue lake, surrounded by spikes of mountain and dark green forest. The surface of the lake is still, and now that we've stopped clomping, I can hear all the forest sounds—the wind blowing through the trees, birds chirping, something that sounds like a frog.

He hoists his pack down and helps with mine.

"It's beautiful."

"You're beautiful."

I tear my gaze from the lake to discover his eyes on my face. He takes a step toward me.

I back away. I'm filthy and disheveled. There are leaves in my hair. My gray Lady Gaga shirt is drenched in sweat and smeared with peanut butter and dirt. My socks are damp, my feet blistered—

"Don't you dare try to kiss me," I warn. "I am so disgusting . . ."

"You are glorious."

I think he might mean it.

"You're crazy."

"You hiked six miles. Aren't you proud of yourself?"

"No. I'm crazy, for agreeing to this."

"Take off your shirt."

I glare at him.

"Take off all your clothes."

The bossiness is secretly very sexy, but no way am I admitting that. "Chase, I am the grossest I have ever been in my whole life. There is no way I am having sex with you."

"We're not having sex. Take off your clothes."

When I hesitate, he does it for me, peeling me out of my smelly, awful shirt that I may have to burn in the campfire tonight, rolling down my shorts—because they are so wet and sticky that they won't slide.

"That is not camping underwear."

I'm wearing black boy shorts with lace trim and a black lace bra.

His voice is stern, but his eyes are approving. It's a good combo on him.

"I like beautiful things. So sue me."

"I like beautiful things, too." His gaze eats me up.

He grabs his T-shirt at the back of his neck and yanks it over his head in one smooth motion.

I'm not sure if it's that distinctly alpha male gesture or the ripple of his abs that makes me woozy.

He unsnaps and unzips his hiking pants and drops them to the ground. Wearing only his gray knit boxer briefs, he scoops me up—every last tired, sweaty, disgusting bit of me— and, ignoring my protests and kicking, carries me into the lake and drops me in the water.

Every cubic inch of air gets sucked out of my lungs by the cold.

"You bastard!" I sputter, surfacing. "Oh my God, that's cold! I'm going to die of hypothermia."

He dives under, surfaces, and wraps his arms around me. "Let me warm you up. So you don't die of hypothermia."

He's 100 million degrees of smooth skin over bunching muscle. I almost forget to hate him, because I'm so busy pressing myself as close to the heat source as I can.

Almost. "You are an evil, evil man."

"Here's what's good about the icy lake." He ducks his head, slips the cup of my bra down, and takes one rock-hard nipple in his mouth. The contrast between the heat of his mouth and the cold of the lake is electrifying. So electrifying that I shut up, clutch his head, and let him suck my nipples in turn, while his hand slides down the front of my panties. He finds my core with two fingers, his thumb circling my clit.

"God, Liv, you're so hot."

Circling, spiraling, the perfect pressure, the perfect rhythm.

I forget my extreme physical misery and come, thrashing, against him.

He wears the self-satisfied expression he always gets when he makes me come. Cat that swallowed the canary, all the way.

He tromps ashore, digs something from his pack, and returns with some camping soap and a washcloth. "I want you to know that this soap is a concession to you. It feels wrong to get clean on the trail. My ideal is three to four days of uninterrupted sloth and filth."

"Thank you," I say, not particularly graciously. But I get

more gracious as he washes me, gracious enough that I find myself squeezing camping soap into the palm of my hand, cupping his balls in one hand to warm them while I get him off, slippery and slipperier, with the other.

My name echoes very nicely across the surface of the lake.

"Open-air hand job, achievement unlocked," I murmur, making him laugh.

We get out and dry ourselves off with our dirty clothes—sigh—and then get into our warmest things.

"Grateful for a real sweater yet?"

I am, unbelievably cozily grateful, but of course I'm not going to admit it.

"You fell in the lake and you don't have any extra underwear!" he crows.

I have to shake my head and roll my eyes.

We pitch the tent on a flat part of the beach. Okay, Chase pitches the tent while I more or less flap my hands and pretend to be useful. When he's done laying the foam pads and sleeping bags inside, I pull a gauzy scarf from where I shoved it in the bottom of my backpack and hang it across the inside of the door. "Home sweet home." I look at him triumphantly.

"You carried that all the way up here? Why would you—?"

"Just to annoy you—is it working?"

He can't hide his smile.

We gather fallen wood and he builds a campfire on the beach. I watch. I wouldn't have billed myself as a woman who could be snowed by Boy Scout tricks, but watching him kneel, broad-shouldered, and patiently coax flame from a little twirl of smoke—

Is it getting warmer, or is that the newly blazing fire?

We dry our clothes on a branch that conveniently overhangs the fire at a safe distance. He sharpens sticks with his Swiss Army knife (more points for both self-sufficiency and sexiness) and hands me one. As parts of the fire die to coals, we roast hot dogs.

"Where did you get these hot dogs? They're really good."

He laughs. "That's the camping talking. Everything tastes amazing after a day on the trail. They're just Oscar Mayer grocery-store hot dogs."

Seriously, it's the best hot dog ever.

The sun goes down while we're eating—thank you, amazingly long Pacific Northwest summer days!—and the air's cold now. I drag our sleeping bags down near the fire and climb into mine, wrapping it around me waist high. In the dark, it's like something out of a book, the two of us sitting next to the fire, flames licking bright and cheerful. He gets out the s'mores makings and we spear marshmallows. Predictably, I suck at making s'mores and he has Eagle Scout–level skills. Two of mine go up in flames while he produces golden-brown perfection. He sandwiches it with a piece of dark chocolate between two half graham crackers, opens his mouth wide while I watch, drooling . . .

Then holds it out to me, intact. "Just kidding. It was always for you."

Oh, my God, it's good. I mean, gourmet good. Why don't they serve this in restaurants more often as dessert? Like a big pan of graham crust with melty marshmallow and chocolate.

"O face," Chase says, as I pop the last bite of s'more in my mouth.

His eyes are dark.

"What?"

"You make an O face when you eat something you really love."

Something about the firelight slows time down, so when he leans in to kiss me I have an eternity to deliciously anticipate.

36

CHASE

Liv kisses me like I'm essential for her survival, like I'm food and oxygen both at once. Her mouth is sweet with marshmallow and chocolate, and her tongue tangles with mine like we're wrestling. Something about the challenge of that gets me going, same as when we spar with words. It's like I have to get the better of her, and in this case, that means I have to kiss her into submission. Kiss her till she can't remember her name, or mine, or where we are.

My mouth still on hers, I unzip the sleeping bag that's wrapped around her and spread it under her, easing her down. I release her long enough to open the other bag—

"Come back," she whimpers.

I spread the other open bag over her and begin undressing her underneath it, pants first. She helps.

"Leave your shirt and your sweater on, but push them up. Take your bra off."

"Not wearing a bra," she whispers. "I wouldn't be wearing panties, either, but my camping guru told me to bring only one pair of pants and I didn't want to ruin them the first time you kissed me or touched me or talked to me or—"

I kiss her and remove the panties in question. They're damp, which makes me want to bury my face between her legs, no preliminaries. But I promised I'd eat her out while the cold air pinched her nipples, and I don't want to deprive her of any part of the camping experience.

I tug the top sleeping bag up above her waist and she does as told, leaving her shoulders and belly covered but her breasts bare. Her nipples shrink and tighten in the cold. I kneel, bend close, and take them in my mouth, one, then the other, flicking the hard nubs with my tongue. She moans and clutches my head.

"The one you're not sucking is so cold," she tells me.

"Keep talking," I instruct.

"It's so tight it hurts. And I can feel the tingle all the way down. It's like there's a cord and when my nipple tightens, it pulls on the cord and my clit and my pussy feel it too."

I make a choked sound.

"What is it? Me saying pussy? I don't actually think of it that way," she says matter-of-factly. "I usually say vagina, honestly, but you said pussy, so I figured that's what turns you on. And whatever turns you on turns me on."

"Convenient," I gasp around her breast. My hand circles it while my tongue works the tip, and I'm so mindlessly hard it's all I can do not to rub myself against her thigh, but if I do that I'll be gone in a few good thrusts.

I crawl under the sleeping bag and reposition myself between her legs, the head of my dick—still clothed in boxers and hiking shorts—so close to the pussy in question that I can feel heat radiating. It's hot under the covers, so I throw off my sweater and T-shirt, settling my bare chest against her belly and once again turning my attention to her gorgeous breasts. Overflowing handfuls, dark-tipped, incredibly sensitive—

She moans and thrashes, and I can feel her trying to get a hold on me, trying to get what she wants—friction, pressure, something to fill her emptiness. I slide farther down, breathing heat over her skin until I can tease my nose against her slit, her salty scent overwhelming my senses. I flick my tongue along the seam, and she cries out. I return my hands to her breasts, pinching her nipples hard, flicking them, while I let my tongue tease so lightly at her mound that it must be driving her fucking mad.

"Chase," she begs.

There's something so excellent about Liv begging. About Liv, who is so strong and so sure, reduced to this. So I do it more. I tease and tease, my tongue outlining the cleft over and over again, finding her clit more swollen with each pass but only barely touching where she needs me most.

"I hate you hate you hate you hate you hate you," she chants, as I take my hands away from her breasts to part her lips, licking everywhere except her clit, teasing in circles that close in but won't complete, making sure I touch every last sensitive surface with my lips and tongue. She lifts her hips and thrusts toward my face, she grabs my head and pushes, but I keep her right here, desperate and on the edge.

Then I raise myself up on my elbows and pull the edge of the sleeping bag back so I can see her face.

She glares down at me.

"Do you want to come?"

"Yes, I fucking want to come."

"Would you be willing to ask for it?"

"I want to come."

"You can do better than that."

"I'm going to get you back for this," she says.

"I have no doubt," I tell her dryly.

"Please, Chase. Please make me come."

I squint at her. "More feeling."

I resume my teasing, one hand once again circling her breasts but this time refusing to even touch the sensitive points, my other hand holding her open so I can apply the warmth of my mouth everywhere she wants me except her swollen clit.

"Please, Chase," she begs, sounding much more like she means it. "Please, please, please—please make me come. God, Chase, you are such a fucking sadist, pleeeeeease!"

I oblige with an open-mouthed kiss to her pussy, my tongue circling in on its target, both my hands finding both her nipples, pinching, flicking, tweaking, until she's thrashing under me and sobbing: "Yes, yes, yes, yes, yes oh my God, yes."

It takes a while before she says anything else.

"This was a good day," are the first words out of her mouth.

It wasn't just a good day. It was a perfect day. Hiking in the woods. Eating by the side of a stream. Making camp by a lake. The swimming, the campfire, the hot dogs, the marsh-mallows.

This.

She clutches my arm. "I love this." She gestures around us —the orgasm, yes, but also the campfire, the lake, the starry sky, the whole fucking forest—her sweep takes in all of it. "I didn't think I would, but I do."

I open my mouth. I'm not sure what I think is going to come out. I've done it, what I set out to do. I have made her love what I love, and surely, surely that means—

I love you.

Stay with me.

I open my mouth.

"Did you hear me?" she teases. "I admitted I like something you like. Aren't you supposed to lord it over me?"

I stare at her.

Just say it. Just say it.

"Chase," she whispers.

She's lying there, holding her arms out to me.

"Mmm-hmm?"

"I feel empty. I want you to fill me up."

Oh, God.

Every single last thought flies out of my head.

I seat the swollen head of my cock against her wet heat, and press deep.

At first, she is sleepy and languid and relaxed under me, which is unbelievably sexy. Every time I push into her, she releases a soft little half-moan, and her breasts jiggle. Her mouth is open and her lids are at half-mast, and I think, I could do this all night.

But then at some point, her little half-moans break open into full moans, and her pussy starts gripping and squeezing me again, and she pulls her knees up and pushes her hips up and starts rocking to meet me—and that's unbelievably sexy, too.

Everything Liv does is unbelievably sexy.

I wish I'd known. There's so much I wish I'd known about her. If we'd gotten together sooner, maybe I could have kept her from wanting to leave.

But right now, I can't think about the past or the future. I can only think about heat and wetness, how red her mouth is, how blue her eyes are, how tight she is around me, the rhythm we've agreed on without any words, which is perfect, the perfect speed, the perfect depth—all of me, to the hilt, my balls meeting her body on every stroke so it's like its own caress, sweet Jesus. Everything falls away—regret, fear, the forest, the sky, the rough ground beneath her—until it's just the two of us, and then, when her jaw tightens and her eyes open wider with wonder and I know she's going to come again, and I let myself tumble over the edge to meet her, even that distinction fades, and for a long, sweet moment, we're one.

37

LIV

I'm missing something. Something important. I'm in a hallway. Long. Vaguely familiar. Lined with bedrooms. Each bedroom, a child. Each child, vaguely familiar. But it's confusing. The children don't all belong together. The rooms don't all belong together. The hallways don't lead where I think they should lead. I wander. It gets darker. I hear sirens. The police will come and take me away and I'll never find the thing that's missing. I hurry, hurry, hurry, but I hear the door downstairs fly open, I hear the sound of voices, footsteps on the stairs, they appear at the top of the stairs, uniformed and faceless. I turn to run but they grab me . . .

"Liv. Liv!"

I'm struggling. I'm crying.

"It's me. It's Chase. You're okay. You were dreaming."

I'm panting, sobbing, but I recognize his voice, the comfort of his arms, the tent around us, the woods beyond. We're camping, and I had a nightmare, and he's here.

"What were you dreaming?"

"A house. One I know but don't know, made up of all the

places I've lived. There are rooms from all my foster homes, and kids from all my foster homes. And then the police come and take me away. I don't know why; I just know I can't stay. And it's important to stay."

His voice is quiet in the deep dark and stillness. "Do you have it over and over?"

"Mmm-hmm. I have other nightmares, too. But this is the recurrent one."

It happens, also, to be the one I was having the night Zeke asked me to move in with him. Which adds an extra layer of choking sensation to the panic that grabs me when I wake from the dream.

But I don't want to think about that. I want to shut out the unwanted images, the bad memories. I want to drown them in my good feelings for Chase. So I turn into his embrace and raise my face. It's too dark to see, but I can feel his breath moving across my face.

"Liv," he whispers.

"Make it go away," I say, and he does.

ON THE HIKE back to the car, Chase teaches me another dumb camping song he learned from his uncle as a kid, and we sing it at the top of our lungs.

Black socks, they never get dirty
The longer you wear them the blacker they get
Sometimes, I think I should wash them
But something inside me keeps saying NOT YET . . . NOT YET
. . . NOT YET.

We've just fallen silent when we emerge into the parking lot, slaphappy, ridiculous, and smelly.

Sometime on Sunday, I stopped caring about the pains in my body or the sad shape of my personal hygiene. By Sunday night, I was so happy to eat the strange brew of rice and beans that Chase fed me that I waxed rhapsodic about it all the way through the meal. And later that night, I was so ecstatic to be horizontal on the ground and headed toward dreamland that I couldn't have cared less that my little rectangle of territory was hard and rocky.

I sleep all the way back to Chase's house in the car, and wake only when he pulls into the driveway. It feels like I'm surfacing from ten feet under.

"The only thing better than camping is the first shower afterward," Chase declares, as he shoulders his pack—and mine—into the house. All I can do is stagger behind him and feel grateful that I don't have to carry the pack even ten feet more.

"Do you want to go first?" I ask, not because I am being gracious but because I know I will take waaaay longer than he does.

"We can both go," he says suggestively, but I roll my eyes at him. Sex is not compatible with my current physical state.

Which is not to say it's not on my mind.

Katie is with her grandmother until tomorrow morning, so it's only the two of us in the house. I'm grateful for that, because there are only three more nights before I drive to Golden. And even though we had really amazing sex on Saturday night and even more phenomenal sex Sunday night after a romp through a waterfall, I am still wanting more.

Still, I'm in no condition to share a small space—yet. "You

go first," I say, and he doesn't try to argue with my assertion that it would be sexier for us to get clean first and be happily naked together after, which I take as a sign that I stink as bad as I think I do.

So, after he goes, I have a blissful, steamy, solo experience of sloughing off two days of dirt and, um, scent. I spend quality time with my flat iron and even put on a little bit of mascara and lip gloss because I can. Then I stand in front of the mirror and feel like myself for the first time in three days.

Except the truth is, I felt surprisingly much like myself hiking those trails with Chase, sleeping out with him at night.

Not that I won't really enjoy making him take me to a schmoofy restaurant where he will have to put his napkin on his lap and order in either French or Italian.

The thought makes me smile.

I head downstairs and find him slouched on the couch, watching something on his iPad.

"Did you have a blissful reunion with your personal grooming products?" Chase looks up. "Oh, wow. Yeah, you did." He runs his gaze over me and gives an appreciative wolf whistle. "You clean up really nice." He holds out both hands, takes mine, and tugs me toward him.

The doorbell rings.

"Who the f—? On a Monday night? At dinnertime?"

I get up and cross to the door. I open it, and a woman is standing there, wearing a pencil skirt and silk blouse. She's tall and slim, with jet-black hair and beautiful green eyes, rimmed with smoky makeup.

I feel a hot, dirty flare of jealousy.

I have no idea who is she is, but I hate her, instantly.

You have no right to hate her, Liv, a little voice says.

He's not yours.

You're not staying.

And then it hits me: I'd let myself forget.

I'd let myself forget I was leaving.

And this:

This is what happens when you stay too long.

Something shows up at the door to remind you that it's time.

And suddenly it's all over me, the itch, the sense that's almost panic: Time to go.

"Liv?" the woman asks. She sounds confused, and now I'm confused, too. Because she knows my name. "It's Gillian. Gillian Hollis. I'm Eve's friend. We had an appointment?"

And then I recognize her.

My replacement. Literally. Katie's new nanny.

"Gillian!" I say, her name falling out of my mouth as my social self takes over.

"Liv?" Chase asks behind me.

"It's the nanny candidate I told you about. I forgot we'd said tonight—I'm so sorry, Gillian, it's been a while and I didn't recognize you at first. But come in! Come in."

"I thought I might have the wrong day!" she says, stepping forward to hug me.

"Oh, God, I'm so sorry! I never put it my calendar, but we're fine! We're both here, and it's Chase you really need to talk to, anyway."

Chase rises from the couch and steps forward. He sees her, and I watch his face to see his reaction. And then I hate myself for caring.

He extends a hand and they shake politely.

"This is Gillian Hollis. Chase Crayton."

"Maybe we should postpone this?" Chase asks, looking to me, a question in his eyes.

"Why would we do that?" I ask. Because I'm on the brink of hiring my replacement, of getting out of Chase's house and hair, of moving on with my life.

That's what this was always about. Always for.

Getting out of Revere Lake.

Before he can answer, I say, "No, let's do this! You need a nanny, and it's time for me to get to Golden."

"I'm happy to postpone, if you need to," Gillian says gently, looking from one of us to the other.

"No need for that," I say. "We're good to go now. Actually. I'm not even sure you guys need me? I've just been filling in for Chase's last nanny. Chase is the real expert on Katie."

"Stay," Chase says.

His eyes are on my face, and there's something in them that's soft and eager—so un-Chase-like it takes my breath away.

For a second my heart races out of control.

Stay.

"Liv is great with Katie. You'll want to get her take on things," he tells Gillian.

And I realize: No amount of wishful thinking will change the fact that it's time for me to go.

38

CHASE

Gillian seems great. She is polite and professional. She asks questions about Katie—about her eating habits, her preferences, her health—and about me, and what I want for Katie. She talks enthusiastically about how she loves outdoor activities and crafts and introducing kids to music, theater, sports, dance, and whatever else they're interested in.

I haven't seen her with Katie yet, of course, but I can imagine that Gillian will be great with her. Katie will love that Gillian knows how to do twelve different kinds of French braids and has memorized the lyrics to all the *Frozen* songs.

So why don't I feel any enthusiasm at all about the possibility of hiring her?

It's a rhetorical question. I know exactly why. It's because I don't want to hire a new nanny at all.

I want Liv to stay.

"Katie really loves crafts," Liv says to Gillian. She's leaned in chummily, hands on knees, all smiles. "I've been teaching her to make friendship bracelets and lanyards and a bunch of other relatively simple thread-craft. I think she might be ready for some sewing, even. She's got very good hand-eye coordination."

She says it with pride.

"And I've been teaching her some simple cooking and baking, too, and she loves that. We even separated eggs and beat the whites the other day and she only broke one yolk."

"That's amazing for five!" Gillian says.

"I know, right? The only thing we really haven't talked much about is sleep." She hesitates, turning to me. "Do you want to tell Gillian about the nightmares?"

No.

No, I don't want to tell her about Katie's nightmares.

Liv's so lighthearted, as if leaving Katie, turning her over to someone else's care, were no big deal. As if leaving, period, were no big deal. But I have no right to be petulant. I knew from the very, very beginning that Liv wasn't staying.

Still, it doesn't make this feel any better.

"I don't know if Liv mentioned, but Katie lost her mother about two months ago."

"Oh," Gillian says, stricken. "I'm so sorry."

"Thank you," I say. "We weren't married, or particularly close, but you can imagine how hard it's been for Katie. She still occasionally has nightmares. But if you go in and comfort her, she settles down fast. She'll just go back to sleep. Otherwise she's a really good sleeper. No night terrors or waking up and wanting to be out of her bed or any of that. No bed-wetting."

"And I'd be fine if there were," Gillian says, beaming reassuringly. "I've dealt with that before. I actually did the bed-wetting alarm with the previous family I worked with, and I got up with the kids at night and everything. Two weeks, and no more bed-wetting."

She smiles at both of us. She really is very competent.

I will be lucky to have her.

I repeat it to myself, for reinforcement: I will be lucky to have her.

Liv and Gillian are chatting away again, about dress-up chests and making magic wands with dowels and card stock and glitter . . .

My mind wanders back to that day when Liv and Katie and I played make-believe together. How hard I laughed when Liv insisted frogs didn't talk. The expression on Liv's face when Katie informed her that she was the ugly, ugly frog. Liv's mini-lecture on inner beauty. The moment Liv and I locked eyes and pretended to fall madly in love.

"Chase? Do we have any more questions for Gillian?"

I wrench my attention back to the present moment.

"Um, no, I think we're all set."

Liv shoots me a puzzled glance. "Okay, then," she says. "Guess that's it for now. We'll be in touch about asking you to come meet Katie, right, Chase?"

"Um, yeah. We'll—I'll—be in touch about next steps. Thanks for coming by, Gillian. We're—I'm—very impressed by what you bring professionally."

We walk her to the door.

As soon as she's gone, Liv turns on me, face screwed up with confusion. "What was that about? You sounded like a robot. Don't you like her?"

"I like her fine."

"So why were you such a dick to her?"

"I wasn't a dick. I just—"

I don't want you to go.

Don't go.

"I can't believe you're so cavalier about leaving her."

The words pop out of my mouth.

Damn it!

That wasn't what I meant to say. Not at all.

What I really meant was, *I can't believe you're so cavalier about leaving us.*

What I really meant was, *I can't believe you're so cavalier about leaving me.*

What I really meant was, *Please don't leave me.*

She gets a look on her face like she's been slapped. "You think this is easy for me? No way. It's really hard. I love Katie. I don't want to leave her. But you knew all along that's what was going to happen. Don't make me feel guilty about it now. I'm trying to make it as easy for you guys as possible. And I don't owe you anything here, Chase. We made a deal. I took a job from you. You wanted me to watch her. You could have hired someone else and eliminated this whole transition, but you asked me to step in. So cut the crap."

She's mad. Really mad. And of course, she's a hundred percent right. I have no right to be mad at her this way. Especially not when I know who I'm really mad at, and what I'm really mad about.

She crosses her arms. "You knew I was going to leave."

She's fired up—cheeks pink, eyes sparkling, breath coming fast. And I shouldn't be thinking about the other times when she's looked like that, but she's reprogrammed my brain and body to want her. Need her. All the time. I can't ignore those feelings.

I won't ignore those feelings.

"I did. But things have changed." I take a deep breath. "I want you to stay."

He wants me to stay.

He wants me to stay.

"You want me to stay . . ." I ask cautiously, " . . . for Katie's sake?"

He shakes his head. "For my sake. Because of this thing between us. That neither of us was planning on or counting on, but Liv, you know it's happening, right? I mean, this is real. I don't know what it is yet, but I don't want you to walk away."

I don't want you to walk away.

There's a swelling sensation dead center of my chest, a buoyancy, and for a moment I ride it.

I don't want to walk away.

I want to stay.

It's an old, almost forgotten feeling.

Stay here.

Home.

Where my people are. Where my things are. Where my life is.

Unpack the contents of the turtle shell. Move them into shelves and drawers. Let myself fill the corners of a place.

Until—

Until someone screws up.

Until someone changes his mind.

Until someone more important, younger, cuter, better . . .

I can see myself not even an hour earlier, frozen at the sight of Gillian in the doorway. How pretty she looked, how much I hated her, how jealous I felt. You can't hold onto the people or things that feel like yours.

They're not yours.

I can see myself as a child, standing in the foyer of one of my foster houses. The third, I think. I stood with one hand on the pull of my suitcase. Everything I owned was in that suitcase. I waited inside the door for the car that was going to come, pick me up, and take me away. Again.

And suddenly the pressure in my chest isn't buoyant, it's suffocating. Like I've taken a deep breath but it's turned out to be seawater.

An anchor can keep you in place or drown you. That was what my foster sister used to say, the one who taught me about carrying my shell on my back.

I'm shaking my head. Almost violently.

"I have a job, Chase. In Golden."

"But why Golden, Liv? When you could have a job here? You could be Katie's nanny."

I open my mouth to try to explain, but the truth is, I can't explain. Even I don't fully understand the impulses that keep me moving. The itch, the pull, the need to go.

I only know it feels right to keep moving.

It feels safer to keep moving.

I've been in Revere Lake too long.

Long enough to make friends.

Long enough to form attachments to people and places and things.

Long enough to make mistakes, like this one I am in the middle of.

"It's where this job was."

It sounds so lame.

"I could give you a job."

I shake my head, hard. "I can't stay here and be your nanny—I'd hate myself for that, and resent you."

He's shaking his head, too, his face bright, excited, hopeful, an awful contrast to the dark weight pressing me down. "You don't have to be my nanny. Gillian could do that. Or anyone. I could—listen, what about this. This is what I'm thinking. If I win the business plan contest and buy the store, I could hire you to keep working on the stuff we were doing the other night. The weekend teaser programs and the coupons. You could get another nanny position, with another family, and do the store stuff part-time—"

"No. I can't."

He exhales sharply.

"I can't—I can't stay. And that would be weird anyway. I don't have retail or marketing experience. People would think you were just doing it because you were sleeping with me."

He looks away. I've hit the target dead center.

He takes a breath, squares his shoulders, finds my gaze again. "So forget the part about the store. We'll figure it out. You'll find something. Just don't go to Golden. Liv, I don't want you to go."

"You think that now."

"I know that now."

"Chase," I say sternly. "I have known you for almost three years. And in that time, you've never been serious about anyone. You'll get bored of me, the same way you get bored of them. And we'll hate each other because you'll have kept me here, and I'll have kept you from being free. And the thing is, Chase, I never want you to hate me."

As I'm saying it, I know I'm right. It will be so hard to walk away from Katie and Chase now. But if I stick around and then it doesn't work out, it will be so much harder. Because then I would be walking away from everything. A family. A job. A home. Belonging.

I can't do it again.

"I wouldn't. This is different. You're different. To me."

I shake my head. "Chase, I know you think it is, but people don't change that much. They think they will, they think they want to, but they don't. You're the guy you are, and I don't want you to have to change that for me."

Chase's face has gone blank.

The house is so quiet, I can hear the refrigerator humming. Rain begins to fall, gently, outside. My own heartbeat thrums in my ears.

"No," he says, at last. "You're right. People don't change. Not in the way you mean."

They're the words I wanted to hear, but as soon as they're out of his mouth, I realize that I was hoping against hope that he'd say something else.

I'll change. For you.

Stay, and I promise I will love you forever.

But he didn't say either of those things.

He doesn't seem angry. Sad, maybe, like me. Because it's

been so good. Because if we were different people, in a different situation, this might be the answer.

As if he can read my mind, he says, "Are we still friends?"

"Of course."

Wrinkles form in the bridge of his nose. "What kind of friends? The kind you stay in touch with when you leave?"

I hesitate, and in that moment, the blankness behind his expression gets even deeper. Like the stillness in the world after an ice storm.

"No," he says decisively. "Not that kind."

40

CHASE

Liv comes into the living room where I am sitting and trying to convince myself that I am finishing up my business plan. What I am really doing is staring blankly at the screen. It could be anything—the Declaration of Independence, a thriller, porn—and I'd still be staring at it blankly, because my brain is submerged in a freezing fog, like the stuff that drifts over the Seattle area in January.

"Do you want me to write some cheat sheets for Gillian before I go?" Liv asks me.

"Sure."

She takes a breath. "She's going to be great."

"Yeah. She seems really, um, yeah . . . great."

Yeah. That's about where I am right now. Freezing fog.

She stands there for a beat. Trying, I know from personal experience, to find something to say that will make things okay between us. But there isn't anything.

It's Wednesday night now, and this is how it's been since Monday night. Liv leaves tomorrow morning.

The world keeps doing its thing. Liv met Emily midway

on Tuesday to retrieve Katie. Gillian came to the house this morning and met Katie. As predicted, they got along great. They did a *Frozen* sing-along and a craft project and at the end, I offered Gillian the job and she accepted.

I'm almost done with the business plan, and I think it's good. It's not shiny and polished, but it's chock full of ideas and I've been over the numbers a hundred times—they're solid. And best yet, it feels like it's in the spirit of what Mike has always wanted the store to be—part of the larger community of outdoorsmen.

But even with all the good things that are happening, I feel like I'm going through the motions. I feel like Robot Chase, who puts one foot in front of the other and says the right things but isn't really present.

Maybe I should have argued harder with Liv. Maybe I should have begged her not to go.

But I've tried that before. I've begged for what I wanted: my parents' business, Thea's love, more time with Katie. And all that happened was I lost what I was begging for, and a little bit of myself, too. I won't do it again.

Not even for Liv.

41

LIV

Even though she's known it was coming, Katie flips out when it's time for me to say goodbye.

"But I don't want Liv to leave. She's the best with my nightmares! She's the best with making a table! She's the best with helping me shop for things! She's the best with singing 'Let it Go'! She's the best with getting library books!"

She starts to cry. My own tears spill over, and I do my best to swat them away before she can see.

"I don't want another new mommy!"

For the first time since our conversation Monday night, Chase makes eye contact with me. His expression is utterly stricken, and I'm flooded with guilt. I never, ever should have said yes to this setup. Look what I've done. I've made Katie's transition harder; I've ruined a friendship.

But what's done is done. The past is rearview, and I have to keep moving forward. It's the best thing for me and it's definitely the best thing for Katie.

"I'm not your mommy," I say as gently as I can. "I'm your nanny. And you'll love Gillian. She'll be your new nanny, and she'll come soon and play with you. You'll have such a good time with her. Nannies come and go, Katie. They don't stay forever. But your daddy will always be your daddy. And he is a really great daddy. You are super lucky."

Chase's face has that same blank look it got the other night when we were talking about me staying. When he realized I was right and there was no way he could promise me what I needed. But he gathers himself, pulls himself together, for Katie's sake. A deep breath, and he kneels to face Katie at eye level.

"That's right, baby. I will always be your daddy. And I will help you with all those things. Singing 'Let It Go' and even going shopping and helping you make a table," he says.

I wait for him to cast me an eye roll, something, but he is entirely focused on Katie. And for some reason, that's when it really sinks in, that I have lost him. We will not kid around anymore about the ways we are different and the shit that bugs him about me and the shit that bugs me about him. I won't teach him hairstyles and marketing techniques, and he won't teach me how to camp or cast or whatever you call what you do with fishing line. We won't spar or kiss or make love or watch different movies side by side.

It's over.

Oh, Chase.

I knew this would be hard. I just didn't know it would be this hard.

Katie tugs my sleeve. "Livvy. Why do nannies come and go? Why do you want to be a come-and-go person instead of a stay person?"

Oof.

I open my mouth to try to explain, when there is no way

to explain it at all, but Chase says gently, "Liv has to go to Golden to take a new job."

"She has a job here," Katie pouts.

"Well," Chase says. "Yes. But she likes to travel and see different places. And she deserves to have a chance to do that. And for that, she needs to go to Golden. And we need to let her go, because that is one of the things you do when you love someone. You let them go be who they need to be."

Tears fill my eyes, but I blink them back.

I am determined not to cry, because it will only make things harder for Katie.

Gillian arrives as I am packing the car. She's brought a tub of little troll dolls and a stack of different-colored pieces of felt and some kid-friendly scissors. She gets down on the floor and shows Katie how to cut holes in the felt to make rudimentary troll clothes. Katie is enchanted, and before too long, she and Gillian are immersed in their troll world.

I kiss Katie on the top of the head and tell her goodbye. She stops cutting troll outfits long enough to hug me, then throws herself back down on the floor.

I walk with Chase to the door.

"I'll walk you to the car," he says.

We walk to the curb, where my new old car is parked. I bought it with the fifteen hundred dollars that Chase paid me.

I put my suitcase in the trunk.

"I guess this is goodbye," he says.

"Yeah."

I want to hug him. I want to throw my arms around him and feel the warm solidity of his body against mine. I want to tell him that I don't want to go, that if I could just believe...

But I can't.

We stand there awkwardly for a moment, and then I get in the car.

I wave to him through the window. He waves back, his gaze faraway and impersonal.

I almost get out of the car. But I don't know what I'd say.

You're the best friend I've ever had.

These have been two of the best weeks of my life.

I wish things were different.

I'd stay if I could, but I can't.

When I'm out of sight, I pull over to the side of the road and burst into tears.

I'm fucked.

Mike's nephew, Whittaker, is standing at the front of the conference room. We're at the offices of Mike's friend Stew, who's the business consultant who's judging Mike's business plan contest.

Whittaker is everything I'm not. He's six four—at least—with neatly trimmed dark hair. Clean-shaven. Wearing an expensive suit. He's hyper-confident—the kind of guy who talks with his hands and makes extra long eye-contact. His handshake was firm but not crushing.

He knows how to play the game.

His Power Point slides are beautiful. They look like they were made by someone with a graphic design background.

Mike and Stew are watching him wide-eyed and admiring, and I'm just sitting here thinking:

I'm fucked.

Because if Whittaker buys the store, it's pretty damn hard to imagine he'll keep me on there.

Whittaker is using phrases and acronyms I've never heard before. Competitive advantage. Paradigm shift. Data-driven. ROI. Core competency.

And Mike and Stew are eating it up.

I want to get up and walk out.

But as I'm sitting there, something happens.

I hear a voice in my head.

Liv's.

When you're working on this business plan, you have to remember that. That you're not the guy your dad said all that shit to anymore. Not at all.

I sit up a little straighter.

I think about how good it felt to work with her, the total flow of the two of us brainstorming and capturing ideas, like two streams merging into one mighty river.

And I force myself to listen to what Whittaker is saying. Like, *really* listen.

And the thing is?

He's not saying that much.

A lot of it's empty.

Like, he's talking about the store's buying decisions being more data driven, but he hasn't said how we'll capture better data. He hasn't talked about replacing our current shitty point-of-sale system or how we could capture more information about our customers. Whereas in my business plan, I address both those issues. He hasn't touched on the online store, or talked at all about partnerships or growing the audience to be anything other than local.

He looks good, and he sounds good...

But I have more substance.

My heart feels half wrenched out of my chest, because I

don't know if there will ever be someone else who has as much faith in me as Liv does.

But just because she went away doesn't mean what she believed about me isn't true.

Whittaker has finished his presentation and is taking questions. There are quite a few, and he fields them handily —but without providing a lot more really useful information. And now I can see that Mike and Stew aren't as completely enamored as I thought. They're withholding judgment, testing whether Whittaker can fill in the blanks...but not ready to fall in love just yet.

"Chase?" Mike asks. "You ready to take your shot?"

I stand up, smile at Mike and Stew—making good solid eye contact—and I say, "Hell, yes, I am."

THE DOORBELL RINGS. I get up from the couch long enough to open the door, then sink back down in front of my glass of bourbon. It's my third. Or fourth. Or maybe fifth.

Brooks and Sawyer are standing there. Brooks strolls over the threshhold, followed by his grim brother, and stands beside me, forehead wrinkled. "You look like the walking dead, Chase. What the fuck?"

"I didn't invite you guys over."

"No, we came over because we're worried about you. You won your business plan contest and instead of being happy, you looked like you were going to puke."

Yes, I won the business plan contest. Mike agreed to sell me the store.

And all I wanted to do was text Liv and let her know.

I wanted to call her and tell her everything—what I'd thought, what I'd said, what Mike and Stew had said.

The look on Whittaker's face when he realized he'd been beaten by a guy with no college education in a pair of jeans and a fishing t-shirt.

But I couldn't, because not only did Liv not want to stay in Revere Lake—she didn't even want to stay in touch.

"You looked happier when you were in the middle of that fight with Thea about where Katie was going to spend Christmas," Brooks observes.

"I'm happy."

"Happy dudes don't drink by themselves," Brooks points out.

"There are more glasses in the kitchen. Right of the sink."

He rolls his eyes, but crosses to the kitchen and comes back with two empty lowballs. He pours himself and Sawyer some bourbon and the two of them sit on either side of me.

I realize that despite Sawyer's dark, silent schtick, I find him weirdly comforting. Like he absorbs everyone else's bullshit.

"You going to tell us what's wrong?" Brooks demands.

"No."

Brooks, wise man, stays silent. Around us, the house is making its night noises, the refrigerator humming, the joists expanding and contracting. I've heard quite a bit of the night noises recently, during the not-sleeping portions of the last three nights, which is pretty much all of them.

Normally, when I can't sleep, I make Liv come watch movies with me. Yes, it's true: I have actually made up nonexistent dates just to have the excuse for one of our consolation parties.

And somehow it never occurred to me that that might be indicative of a problem.

Not too bright, this guy.

Brooks is still eyeing me like I'm a ticking time bomb. "Does this have something to do with Liv's leaving?"

Outright lie? Half-truth? Silence?

"Leave him alone," Sawyer says.

The brothers exchange glances, and Brooks apparently wins, because he nods and says, "You know what? You don't even have to answer that. I know it has to do with Liv's leaving. That's what Rodro guessed. He said you were in love with her. Is that true?"

He asks it the way you'd ask a close friend to confirm the rumor of a cancer diagnosis.

I open my mouth to deny it, because a long time ago, I decided I would never let the phrase "in love with her" apply to me again. But now that Brooks has let it drop like a bomb in my living room, I can see it's true.

That it's probably been true all along.

I think of Liv when I first saw her in Rodro's living room. How beautiful and polished she was, how even then I wanted to feel every curve and secret of her, and how that scared the shit out of me, because the only other time I'd wanted that before, it had landed me in sewage.

All I can do is nod.

Brooks opens his mouth and I think he's going to howl with laughter, but then he seems to realize that I'm in no condition to be laughed at and shuts it again. "We're talking about the Liv who—and I quote—is your friend 'like you and Rodro and I are friends'?"

I have to rest my forehead briefly in my hands.

"Chase, you okay?"

That, surprisingly enough, is Sawyer, and when I lift my head, he's looking at me with eyes that aren't nearly as cold or relentless as I would have guessed. They're gentle.

"No. I'm not okay. I'm definitely not okay." Pretty sure, in fact, that I feel less okay as time passes.

"What happened? How the fuck—" Brooks seems to suddenly realize that we have a genuine humanitarian crisis on our hands. "How do you get from 'just friends' to . . . this?"

His gesture takes in the mostly empty bottle, the mostly empty glass, my trashed living room, and me.

He looks pretty freaked out, too, as if something like this could happen to him if he let his guard down.

I tell the brothers about how Liv and I became friends. How from the very beginning, the two of us put plenty of distance between us. We wouldn't hook up. There were lots of things about us that made us incompatible—the foods we liked, the activities we liked, the fact that neither of us was a candidate for long-term happiness. I even loved that we couldn't agree on a movie because it put all that space between us on the couch. It meant there was never anything shared between us that could pull us together.

And then . . .

"I hired her to come help me with Katie. Why do you think I did that?"

Brooks looks, if possible, even more freaked out.

"I don't know, dude. Because you're an idiot?"

"Thanks, man. That helps."

Saywer clears his throat and holds out the bourbon bottle to me.

Now there's a real friend.

I pour another bourbon, and let Brooks' rhetorical question drop.

I cry most of the way to Boise, and then I dry my eyes, fix my makeup, and check myself into a motel.

I've always liked motels. You decide when to arrive and when to leave, and by definition, they are places you can't stay long. Tonight that fact feels incredibly comforting.

I leave the motel long enough to get dinner. I decide on The Cheesecake Factory, but can't help thinking that Chase would have tried to talk me into Ruth's Chris Steak House. Then we would have made a joke about our incompatibility.

Tears fill my eyes again.

I shouldn't be crying. I'm doing the right thing. I'm taking a job that uses my talents. I'm trying a new city, a place I've never lived before. I'm on the road, on my own, an independent woman who isn't afraid to mold her life into something that's right for her.

I'm taking care of myself, learning from old mistakes, making sure I don't set myself up for heartbreak.

You have to stop crying, I tell myself, and I do a pretty good job of it during dinner. I read the new Sophie Kinsella book and people-watch over the top of my Kindle and eat waaaay too many avocado egg rolls. I leave a big tip and a thank-you note for the waitress, and I depart the restaurant in an excellent mood.

It's a good night. I could spend many happy nights like this.

The only thing that would make it better . . .

But I don't need Chase to watch a movie and drink wine and eat chocolate. I have my iPad, the motel minibar, and a stash of Ghirardelli to meet all my solo movie-watching needs.

So that's what I do. I queue up *La La Land*, which I've been meaning to watch, and I drink wine from a plastic cup and eat most of a bar of 72 percent dark chocolate.

La La Land makes me cry. I know it's one of those love/hate movies—people are crazy about it or it annoys the shit out of them—but it turns out I'm in the love camp.

I feel pleased with myself, afterward. Look. I had a wonderful evening. I was sad, but I still had a good time.

(I managed not to think about how much Chase would have hated *La La Land*, even.)

I'm going to be okay.

I shut down my iPad, clean up my cup and wrapper, and tuck myself into bed. The white-noise whir of the air-conditioning is soothing, and I know I'll fall asleep quickly.

I get out of bed. I need—something. Something important. Not candy. Not ice. I walk down the motel corridor, but it's longer than I was expecting, and the doors of the rooms are open. Each room, a child. Each child, vaguely familiar. But the children shouldn't be here, in the Comfort Inn; that makes no sense. And the hallways don't lead where I think they should lead. I wander. It gets darker.

I hear sirens. The police will come and take me away and I'll never find the thing that's missing. I hurry, hurry, hurry, but I hear the door downstairs fly open, I hear the sound of voices, footsteps on the stairs; they appear at the top of the stairs, uniformed and faceless. I turn to run but they grab me . . .

I wake up and turn in the dark, reaching for Chase.

That's when I realize that there's a whole other gear of heartache that I've been holding at bay. The kind that comes in the middle of the night, when you reach for someone who's not there. When you know that there is a little girl in a house eight hours away who might wake up reaching for you, and who won't understand why you're far away.

When you understand that in trying to avoid the big mistake, you've made the biggest mistake of all.

I cry, and cry, and cry. I cry until I can't cry anymore, until my whole body hurts.

44

CHASE

"Daddy, play with me!"

"In a little bit, sweetheart. I'm working on something."

It's Friday night and I'm being slack about getting Katie to bed. I know I'll miss Liv the most when the house is quiet.

I look up from my laptop and meet the sweetest, bluest eyes you can imagine. Her face has slimmed down but there's still a childish softness to her cheeks, and her blond hair is a messy cloud. My heart squeezes.

I close the laptop. "Let's play, baby."

Katie is an adventurous princess, riding out on her trusty steed to map the kingdom and bring back news from its farthest-flung corners.

She wears her Elsa costume, as well as a piece of silver fabric that Liv got for her at Goodwill, and a crown that she and Gillian made from tinfoil.

Needless to say, I am the horse. I'm a lazy, good-for-nothing horse that frequently loses control of its limbs, unseating its rider and causing lots of hilarity. Even when I am upright, I require lots of prodding and kicking and plying with various forms of horse feed, like magic roses.

I trot all around the living room—er, kingdom—with Katie—er, the princess—on my back, and the princess stops here and there to note something on her map (printer paper, marked up with colored pencil), or to interact with some of her (imaginary) loyal subjects.

Sometimes, if necessary, I fill in for the loyal subjects. Like at one cottage on the very edge of the kingdom, the whole family is sick with Ploogaciriosis, and they're all throwing up a lot. That seems to need dramatization, so I supply it until Katie laughs so hard she runs out of the living room to the bathroom, narrowly averting an accident.

I wish Liv were here. She would be rolling on the floor. I love making her laugh.

Katie has stopped to kiss a whole pond full of frogs, so I take a picture of my princess girl crouched down with her lips pursed, bestowing her favors everywhere. I stand there with my phone in my hand.

There's no point, right? Liv was here with us, we loved her the best we could, and that wasn't enough to convince her to stay. What good will a goofy photo do?

I shove my phone back in my pocket, the photo unsent.

"There are turtles, too, Daddy. Frogs and turtles." Katie bends down to kiss the turtles.

Turtles.

I remember Liv and me, sitting on her bed, in the room she'd transformed. *It's something I learned from one of my foster sisters. She called it carrying her shell on her back.*

She's not a turtle, though. She's a horseshoe crab. She takes a new place and makes it her own.

And then she leaves.

She leaves because—

The only hard part was, I never got to stay. I'd start to feel like I'd settled in, and then something would happen . . . So that's why I loved the idea so much of carrying my house around with me like a shell.

The clockwork of the world grinds to a halt, and in the silence and stillness, I see it, what I've been missing.

She was terrified.

Because every time she'd ever wanted to stay, she'd had to leave.

Because every time she started to feel safe, something went wrong.

Because every time she felt loved, someone took the love away from her.

She left so that wouldn't happen.

Katie is scattering something on the ground.

"What's that, Katie girl?" Liv's nickname for her spills from my lips, without my intending it.

"Bread crumbs," Katie says.

"Why bread crumbs?"

"So we can find our way home. Sometimes if you're in the woods and it's dark and you're scared, you need bread crumbs."

"Yes," I say, although my chest feels like there is a stone on it. "Sometimes you do."

"Daddy, you okay?"

"Yes, Katie girl, I am okay."

It's true. I am sad. I miss Liv more than I can deal with. But I also know exactly what I need to do.

I pull my phone out of my pocket. I pull up the photo of

Katie, with her little pink lips pursed, kissing all the frogs you have to kiss before you find the frog you love best. I click to attach the photo, and then I add text:

Have been doing a lot of thinking. And the thing is: Katie and I? We're your friends, and we're your home. No matter what else happens, we're here. That's a promise. And I don't make promises I can't keep.

I TUCK KATIE IN, read her the tattered copy of *Hi, All You Rabbits* handed down from my mother, and turn out the light.

"Where's Liv now?" she asks.

That's better than what she asked last night, which was, "Is Liv going to come in and say good night?"

I think she'd just forgotten Liv was gone, but for a moment I thought she hadn't understood any of what we'd told her about Liv's leaving, and my chest fissured.

"Liv's probably in . . ." I consult the vague map in my head. "Somewhere in Utah or Wyoming, I'd guess. She'll get to Golden tomorrow."

"I miss her."

"I miss her too."

"Gillian's, nice, though!" Katie says. "She's not the same as Liv, but she's nice."

I've been feeling pretty awful about putting Katie through this. If I'd really thought it through, I would have hired another nanny straight after Celia. One fewer transition for a little girl who needs her life to be stable.

Or would I have?

Did I really hire Liv for Katie's benefit? Or was there a

part of me that had gotten tired of the walls between us and wanted more?

I realize that this is the answer to the rhetorical question I'd asked Brooks the other night. I hired Liv because my subconscious self wanted to tie her to us as long as I could.

Forever if possible.

Only it wasn't.

"I'm glad you like Gillian," I say, ruffling Katie's hair and kissing her soft cheek.

I head downstairs. I'm too mentally tired and burned out to want to do anything other than watch a movie, so I grab my iPad and open the Netflix app.

Hey.

My heart pounds. It's a text from Liv.

That's a cute picture of Katie. Thanks.

Not exactly the response I was hoping for . . . but something. *You're welcome.*

What are you doing?

I think, Missing you. I text, *I was going to watch a movie.*

Which one?

You won't believe it.

Try me.

Wonder Woman.

Chase!

I know, I know. But it does have superheroes and war and explosions. How's the drive so far?

There's a long pause. *Fine. Thinking about watching a movie, too. Maybe For a Good Time, Call . . .*

What's that?

Roommates, phone sex.

She sends me a link to an article.

Chick flicks guys like, huh. OK. I'd watch that.

I was going to ask if you wanted to. Watch it with me, I mean.

I thought maybe you meant have phone sex.

Long silence.

You are so juvenile. Don't make me regret asking you.

I chuckle. *We never watch the same movie.*

I know, but this is an extenuating circumstance.

Extenuating, how?

I'm standing outside your front door.

I OPEN the door and there she is.

She is holding her iPad and she looks so beautiful it makes my heart stop. Her hair is a cascade of copper and her smile, even though it's tentative, is better than sunshine.

"Jesus, Liv, you look good enough to—"

The animal half of me wants to kiss her stupid and get her out of her clothes as fast as possible. The other half of me wants to make this moment last forever. That half wins. I cup her head, feeling the smooth silk of her hair slip through my fingers. I touch her cheek—soft and smooth as satin—and I draw her close, slowly, slowly, slowly, until I can feel her breath against my lips. The burn of our chemistry works its way under both of our skins, and she sighs and slips closer so I can feel the length of her against me, all curves and softness.

I step back, holding her at arm's length.

"You're here."

"I woke up in the hotel in Boise. Checked out. Hit the road, started driving toward Golden. And I realized, I wasn't getting any closer. I was getting farther away. Farther and farther. Each mile. Farther from Katie. Farther from you. Farther from—"

Tears spill down her cheeks.

"Farther from home."

Her bottom lip trembles as she says it.

And I think she's never looked stronger or braver or more beautiful.

"Welcome home," I say, and lower my mouth to hers.

45

LIV

When we pause for breath, I smile at him. "I have some things to say."

Chase raises his eyebrows. "Well, me too."

"When I told you I didn't think you could change, I realized I did exactly what your parents did. And Thea. I assumed I knew who you were and what you'd do in a certain situation, without giving you a chance to prove yourself."

He opens his mouth, but I keep going, because I need him to know. "The truth is, I've never seen you be anything except exactly what I want. Honest and loyal and a terrific friend and an amazing father and—" I bite my lip.

"—seriously, seriously hot in bed," he supplies, crossing his arms.

I smack him.

"I am, though, right?" He does that patented Chase eyebrow waggle that should make me cringe but actually makes the pit of my stomach squirmy. Not that I want him to know that.

"You're supposed to let me say it, asshole."

"So say it," he challenges, leveling me a dark look.

"Best ever. So good. You've spoiled me for every other guy in the universe, and in any parallel universes, and—"

He makes a face. "Don't overdo it. I won't believe you."

"In all seriousness, Chase, if you're serious about asking me to stay, I'm serious about staying."

"Hell yes, I'm serious."

"I didn't get much sleep last night. I was looking up nanny jobs in the Seattle area."

His eyes are warm and soft. "And if you want, I've got a job for you. At the store. I, um, won the business plan contest."

"Chase!" I say, and throw my arms around him, rocking him back and forth.

He gives me a shy, pleased smile, and then he tells me about how his presentation went. How he was intimidated by the other guy, by his polished-ness, but then he heard my voice in his head and knew he could do it.

"I'm sorry I wasn't there for you," I say, because it breaks my heart that I walked out on him when he needed me. "I will be, next time. Every time."

"You *were* there," he says. "Anyway, so, I'm buying the store from Mike. And I'm really fucking excited about it. I know I can do this. I know I'm the guy you see when you look at me. A guy who's good at stuff that matters."

My chest aches and my eyes are all misty. I reach for him, and he pulls me close and clutches me hard against his chest. "I want to stay," I whisper. "Right here."

"Good," he says. "This is where you belong."

He smells like cotton and sweat and I breathe him in, gloriously happy.

"What about the Golden job?"

"Well. Not my finest moment, but when I called to tell them I'd changed my mind, that I'd fallen in love—"

I peek up at his face, not sure what to expect, hoping for the best.

He's smirking. Just a little, just enough. "Say that part again."

"I'm in love with you."

"Again."

"I love you."

He takes a huge breath and sighs it out.

"I love you, too," he says.

Then he bends his head and we spend a few long minutes not being able to get enough of each other.

"Wait," he says, surfacing. "So what happened when you told them you'd fallen in love?"

I grin at him. "They said that they'd just gotten a call that their daycare of choice had an opening, and honestly, they were a tiny bit relieved."

"Well, that's some good fucking luck."

"I think it was the universe telling me to get my ass back to Revere Lake." I touch his face, which is a little bit scruffy, like he hasn't shaved since I left.

"I don't know when I started loving you," I admit. "It might be that I loved you that first night when you showed up at Rodro's and plopped down on the couch like you owned the place."

He makes a noise, like he's going to contradict me, but I put a hand up because I have to get through this; I have to say it all. He needs to know. "And you kept being that way, so honest and so safe. You were the one person who I didn't need anything from so you couldn't take anything away, and then suddenly I did, and that was terrifying, and I couldn't get back to feeling safe with you again, and then when you said you wanted me to stay—"

He sighs. "I should have known you'd freak out. I knew your history. But I—" He looks away. "I never told you this, but when Thea broke up with me, she said something so similar to what you said the other night. That she'd always want me to be more like her, but she knew she couldn't ask me to change for her, that it wouldn't work."

"Oh," I say, stricken. "Oh, God. Chase, no. God, no. I don't want you to be more like me. I love that you're nothing like me. I love that about us, the way we strike sparks, the way we tease, the ways we're nothing alike but somehow fit together."

Quietly, roughly, he says, "Do you know what I want for Katie?"

I shake my head. My throat is tight with unshed tears.

"I want her to grow up to be high maintenance and low maintenance and girly and tomboyish and artsy and sporty and rough and polished and loving action flicks and loving chick flicks and—"

Chase's voice breaks.

I'm crying. I wipe away the tears, but it doesn't help much. I throw my arms around him and he rocks me back and forth, and oh my God, everything fits. Chase, the house, this family —everything wraps around me, and I'm home.

I eventually stop crying and can talk again.

"There's this part at the end of *La La Land*—that's what I watched in the hotel last night—where the whole life he could have had flashes before his eyes. Everything, how it would have been if he hadn't fucked up. And this morning I knew that's how it would be if I kept driving. Every time someone said the word home, this is what I would picture. This living room, you and me watching our movies. Or the dining room with you and me and Katie. Every party I went to, I'd think about the barbecue we had. Every guy who asked me out—"

Chase roars. I don't even think it's actual words, just outrage.

"It's not going to happen! I came back!"

He gives me a dark, dark look: better not.

Mmm. I do so love Chase's possessive thing.

"Anyway, I didn't want to be like the *La La Land* hero anymore, with the life I wanted just a film playing in my mind."

He points a finger at me. "Damn straight. Good thing you came back when you did. I had just about given up on you."

Fear flickers. "You had?"

"Don't be fucking ridiculous," he says, and wraps me up in his arms again.

46

CHASE

"Daddy, why are you making pancakes?"

"I thought you might like some."

"Aren't pancakes just for fesshul occasions?"

"This is a special occasion, Katie girl."

"What occasion?"

"We have a visitor."

Her eyes get really big. "Is it Granna Emily?"

I shake my head. "Nope."

She looks disappointed, but I know she's not going to be disappointed.

I'm not disappointed. I'm totally fucking exhausted, from, well, totally fucking all night long, but I'm the happiest guy on the whole planet. And it makes me even happier to think about how Katie's going to be when she finds out who our visitor is.

"Is it Nana and Papa?"

"Nope."

"Is it Uncle Henry?"

"Nope."

"It's me!" says Liv, appearing in the door of the kitchen, dressed and ready for the day. One thing we did do last night was unload her suitcase from the car. Just that one suitcase. I suspect Liv will never have many permanent belongings, a subconscious hedge against feeling like she might have to move again at any moment. That's fine, as long as she knows that wherever she goes, Katie and I are going with her.

"Livvy, Livvy, Livvy, Livvy, Livvy!" Katie bellows, and throws herself across the kitchen and into Liv's arms.

Katie extricates herself from Liv and eyes her suspiciously. "Why are you here?"

"I'm going to stay here with you and your dad, and I'll get a job here. Your dad thinks I'm going to come work for him, but we'll have to talk about that." She winks at me. We did talk a little bit about it last night. About how we could turn the running of the shop itself over to Brooks and Rodro and work on the online store and partnerships together.

Katie's face is wary. "And you won't leave again?"

It's possible I get a little teary eyed.

A fearful look crosses Liv's face, and I know what she's thinking. Life is uncertain. People leave, they betray you, they make mistakes that separate you from them, they die.

But I will not let her be afraid, not if I can help it.

"You and I, we won't let her, right, Katie girl? Not if it's within our power."

Liv's eyes fill up with tears.

I draw closer to Liv, and tuck her in tight under my arm against my body. Katie sidles closer, too, and when Liv turns her body toward mine and lays her cheek against my chest, Katie makes herself the filling in our sandwich.

We stay like that for a long time.

"You know," Liv tells Katie. "I was getting pretty tired of being a come-and-go person. I think I'm really going to enjoy being a stay person from now on."

"Yay!" says Katie, jumping up and down.

I finish cooking the pancakes and frying up the bacon, while Katie and Liv "make" the table.

I'm done first, while they're still fussing, and I give them a hard time about how the food's getting cold, but I actually like it. Even the little vase of wildflowers that Liv sent Katie outside to pick.

When the table's made, we sit down to eat together as a family.

EPILOGUE

CHASE—MANY MONTHS LATER

You know how there are different kinds of miserable?

Like, there's miserable like Sawyer's been for the whole time I've known him, the kind of miserable you are when your wife has just died.

And then there's the miserable Sawyer is now. Head down on the O'Hannihan's table.

He texted us half an hour ago to see if we wanted to meet up, which maybe should have been my first sign that something was up, because Sawyer never organizes our lunches or nights out. That's Brooks' job.

I checked with Liv to make sure she was okay with putting Katie to bed, kissed both my girls goodbye, and promised Liv I'd be home early enough for us to climb into bed together.

It's my favorite time of day, whether we're making love or just holding hands in the dark. There's something amazing about those moments together, and I feel lucky every night to get to fall asleep next to my best friend.

In the meantime, I'm in the mood to celebrate tonight, so I signal the server for a pitcher. I'm officially the owner of the store formerly called Mike's Mountainwear, now simply called Mountainwear—and I met this afternoon with two new partners, both of whom want to use Mountainwear as the "exclusive provider" of outdoorwear for their trips. I'm more than happy to raise a glass to my day—and to help Sawyer drown his sorrows.

Brooks comes in just behind me, takes one look at his brother, and drops a hand onto Sawyer's shoulder.

Sawyer slowly lifts his head.

"Dude," Brooks says gently.

Sawyer just shakes his head.

Jack arrives at the table, surveys the landscape, then looks to Brooks and me for insight.

We both shrug.

"It's not Jonah, is it?" Brooks asks, sounding about as concerned as Brooks ever sounds. Brooks thinks the sun rises and sets over Sawyer's son—and I'm pretty sure the feeling's mutual.

Sawyer's face gets even darker, if that's possible. "Jonah's *fine*," he says. "He's found his new best friend in the world. They're inseparable."

Sawyer just moved into a new house a few days ago. Brooks and I helped with the move, so I know what Sawyer's talking about—there's a new kid next door, and Jonah hit it off instantly with him. They ran off, talking a mile a minute, and weren't seen again for hours.

"That's *good*, right?" I ask hesitantly, because it's pretty clear it *isn't* good, at least not in Sawyer's book, which makes no sense. Because Sawyer, like me, has been doing everything in his power to help his kid recover from his mom's death, and a new best friend seems like pretty damn great medicine.

Sawyer is shaking his head again as the server brings our pitcher. I reach for it and pour him a brimming glass, and he picks it up and downs half of it before he answers me.

"Normally it would be good. But this kid's mom..."

To my surprise, Sawyer covers his face with both hands.

"Super uptight?" Jack hazards. "Overprotective? Up in your business?"

Still buried in his hands, Sawyer groans. "No," he says. "She's nice. Too nice. Bundle of sunshine nice. Super chatty nice."

"Okaaay," Brooks says slowly. "I can see how that would be a mismatch with your man-of-no-words routine, but that doesn't seem like a reason to have your head down on a table."

"Isleptwithher," Sawyer says.

Sawyer is usually so measured and careful with his words that I don't even realize at first that the rush of noise coming from his covered mouth is a sentence. Then I pick out the individual words.

Jack, Brooks, and I all go mouths-wide-open at the same moment.

"Like—since you moved in?" Brooks' voice cracks from shock.

Sawyer's head shoots up. "No! Hell no! But—it was, I don't know, six months ago. It wasn't even in Revere Lake. It was at Maeve's."

That's a well-known pick-up bar a couple of towns over. It's a good place to go for anonymity, and I know from things Brooks says that one-and-done, anonymous one-nighters is all Sawyer's been interested in for a while. So it's not a surprise that he would have slept with someone at Maeve's.

But holy shit, that's one hell of an unfortunate coincidence.

Jack seems to have put it together first. "So... your one night stand from Maeve's is also your new next door neighbor... and your kid's brand-new BFF's *mom*?"

Sawyer puts his head down on the table again. And bangs his forehead against the surface a few times.

"Wow," Brooks says. "That's some epic bad luck." He brightens slightly. "Or epic good luck, if she was hot and good in bed."

Sawyer raises his head and glares, hard, at his brother.

"Okay, so she wasn't hot and good in bed."

Something flits across Sawyer's face. An expression I would have to interpret as, *she's hot and good in bed, and I really fucking wish she weren't.* As someone who's recently been there, I totally get it.

"It's none of your fucking business," Sawyer growls. "The point is, I'm not sleeping with her again."

Jack's eyebrows go up. Way up.

He looks at me. I look back at him.

We both look at Sawyer.

I know he thinks he means it.

But Jack and I both know he's wrong.

Because Jack and I?

We both have a pretty damn good idea how futile resistance is.

ACKNOWLEDGMENTS

Do Over, *Head Over Heels*, and *Sleepover* were first published in 2018. But re-releasing a book is its own special kind of project, and I have many people to thank with their help in making this edition possible!

First of all, many thanks to my readers for always being along for the ride! I do this for you, and I'm so grateful every time I get an email, message, or smoke signal from the ether telling me these characters have meant as much to you as they have to me.

Mr. Bell and our kids usually get the last place in my acknowledgments, which isn't fair at all, because they have first place in my heart. They're unfailingly patient and supportive and in every way the best family an author—or anyone—could want. I love you all so much.

Thank you so much to Christina Hovland, Brenda St. John Brown, Suzann Goldberg, and Kate Davies for being my awesome readers this time around! Thank you for taking time away from your own work to help make this book the best it could be.

Huge thanks also to the author friends who support me on a regular basis—Dylann Crush, Megan Ryder, Christina, Brenda, Claire Marti, Christine D'Abo, Gwen Hernandez, Rachel Grant, Kate, Kris Kennedy, Karen Booth, Susannah Nix, Stina Lindenblatt, and many, many more, including but not limited to the authors of the Girls' Night In Book Club, the Corner of Smart and Sexy, Small Town World Domination, Wide for the Win, Tinsel and Tatas, and the RAM Rom-Com group.

Thank you to my agent, Emily Sylvan Kim, and my sub rights agent, Tina Shen, who work to make things happen for me behind the scenes!

I cannot imagine doing any of my jobs without the love and support of my amazing friends, Aimee, Chelsea, Cheryl, Darya, Ellen, Gail, Jess, Julia, Kathy, Lauren, Molly, Soomie, and Tracey. Love you!

ALSO BY SERENA BELL

Wilder Adventures

Make Me Wilder

Walk on the Wilder Side

Wilder With You

A Little Wilder

Returning Home

Hold On Tight

Can't Hold Back

To Have and to Hold

Holding Out

Tierney Bay

So Close

So True

Under One Roof

Do Over

Head Over Heels

Sleepover

New York Glitz

Still So Hot!

Hot & Bothered

Standalone

Turn Up the Heat

ABOUT THE AUTHOR

USA Today bestselling author Serena Bell writes contemporary romance with heat, heart, and humor. A former journalist, Serena has always believed that everyone has an amazing story to tell if you listen carefully, and you can often find her scribbling in her tiny garret office, mainlining chocolate and bringing to life the tales in her head.

Serena's books have earned many honors, including a RITA finalist spot, an RT Reviewers' Choice Award, Apple Books Best Book of the Month, and Amazon Best Book of the Year for Romance.

When not writing, Serena loves to spend time with her college-sweetheart husband and two hilarious kiddos—all of whom are incredibly tolerant not just of Serena's imaginary friends but also of how often she changes her hobbies and how passionately she embraces the new ones. These days, it's stand-up paddle boarding, board-gaming, meditation, and long walks with good friends.